Thursday's Child 4

Short Stories by Bay Area Writers

Thursday's Child 4

Short Stories by Bay Area Writers

Edited by
Milton Wolff

Glen Press
Berkeley, California

ACKNOWLEDGEMENTS

A word must be said in appreciation of our own beloved Clara Robbin, Ed's wife, whose courage and dignity in time of tragedy has been a gift to us all. Generously she has continued to provide her home, her time and her practical help, solving our problems and assuring the continuity of the group and the publication of this work.

We wish also to acknowledge the industrious members of the editorial board who put in many hours, both reading alone and in our Saturday morning meetings at Bob Hall's house, working together in a wonderful harmony of spirit. These members include Clara Livsey, Elizabeth Davis, Barbara Crawford, Conrad Montell, Jean MacKellar, Bob Hall and myself as editor in chief. Thanks to the good will of all, the project proved to be a delightful lesson in group dynamics as well as a useful one on the craft of writing.

Milton Wolff

Published by
Glen Press
2247 Glen Avenue
Berkeley, California 94709

Cover illustration by Katy Polony
Cover design by Robert Lee Hall

Typesetting and design by Heyday Books
Printed and manufactured by Edwards Brothers

CONTENTS

1	The Long Ride Back *by Milton Wolff*
11	Take Care of My Cat *by William B. Tenery*
20	Love and Work: Work and Love *by Elizabeth Davis*
26	One Dried Spider *by Kathryn Winter*
35	Sanctuary *by Robert Lee Hall*
43	Dead Boy's Farewell *by Kirsten and Ray Faraday Nelson*
53	Eggs *by Marko*
60	The Brides of Prospect Avenue *by Lili Artell*
72	Excesses *by Jean MacKellar*
80	Green Ribbons *by Clay Fulghum*
87	The Silver Bracelet *by Roselore Fox*
94	Old Glory *by Bruce Kaiper*
101	The First I Love You *by Conrad Montell*
115	The Yellow Mare *by Ruth Broek*
122	White as Milk, White as Cotton *by Lee Ann Johnson*
131	The Mayor's Limousine *by Dexter Mast*
135	The Artist *by Richard Gold*
140	Nothin' But A Bob *by Gwen Jordan*
150	Juan Pedro's High Destiny *by Virginia Ruiz Seiden*
158	Maudie *by Marlin Spike Werner*
164	The Art of Acting Normal *by Nina Clark*
166	Breathe Deeply *by Clara Robbin*
171	Different Strokes *by Ed Robbin*
180	Contributors' Biographies

FOREWORD

This, the fourth volume of short stories to appear under the *Thursday's Child* title, is dedicated to Ed Robbin, who died last April. He was the leader of our group of Bay Area writers. It is not easy to use the past tense when his presence is still so much with us, still influencing the way we conduct our gatherings, the way we think about writing and the way the stories for this book were selected. Ed inspired and was the angel for the first three volumes of *Thursday's Child*. He is the reason there is a fourth. His love of story telling, his eagerness to share with others stories he judged worth the sharing combined with good business sense lead to the production of these collections. Readers have responded enthusiastically and dozens of previously unpublished authors have rejoiced in seeing their efforts in print. To quote one appreciative reader's reaction that is typical:

"Thursday's Child reminds me how much talent the world has walking around, unrecognized and unheralded, [while] there is a tremendous amount of s__t that is foisted on us as 'success' by the establishment . . . ."

Together with his wife Clara, Ed was our host for the group's regular Thursday night readings which involved critiques, bull sessions, coffee and good times. At the old house on Glen Street where we still meet, the vibes were and still are, good. The gatherings are relaxed and informal, but readers and critics alike leave them challenged and inspired by the give and take of the evening.

Ed Robbins was a collector. Not of ostentatious symbols of success, though he had the means to do so, but of stories. Ed loved a good story above most other things. His face glowed with pleasure when one of us read a particularly good story. I would marvel at the enthusiasm with which he would defend a story he admired. His preference was for tales that were "rich . . .a slice of life, peopled with real characters, suspenseful, entertaining and informative . . . ." Stories that met these criteria entered his library whether they were by Sholem Alechiem, Chekov or a member of our group.

Ed also collected people. He collected people on the same basis as he collected stories, individuals who were compassionate and led full lives. He counted among his friends Woody Guthrie, about whom he wrote the book *Woody and Me,* Will Geer, the actor and activist, Nelson Algren and Studs Terkel plus the authors of the stories you find between these pages, their biographies briefly limned in the back pages.

Ed had a gift for affecting the lives of those he gathered around him. In the few years I was with him I witnessed some remarkable changes as he managed, without being heavy-handed about it, to undermine the prejudices of some and smooth out the rough edges of others.

During Ed Robbin's too brief tenure as our leader, several of our group had books published by national publishers. Each chapter had been read aloud, critiqued, and revised with the group's suggestions in mind before it saw print. Many published short stories and essays that went through the same process. At the same time, friendships developed, a few romances flourished and a general selfless comradeship bound us together.

Ed's contribution to the group will not be an easy one to match. That we've carried on well thus far is in no small degree due to the momentum he gave the group. And to this collection. The editorial board responsible for the selection of these 24 stories was determined to make it a volume Ed would have been proud of.

We regret that we were unable to include all the stories submitted to us due to our limited budget, but all of the seventy were good. To make the task of selection less painful the manuscripts were submitted and judged without names. We hope that we carried out our task with the same wisdom, kindness and grace as Ed did earlier, so that those whose stories do not appear will strive to come back stronger next time.

Of course, if there is to be a 'next time' depends on you, the reader. It is only through word of mouth that our books are promoted. If we succeed in pleasing you, we will, in the vernacular of Ed's story "Different Strokes" have kept the faith.

Milton Wolff
El Cerrito
March 1984

THE LONG RIDE BACK
Milton Wolff

Charlie Chaikin sat hunched behind the wheel of his new '61-baby-blue-sun-roof-Beetle VW. He had an important decision to make: *to drive or not to drive—that is the question,* he muttered, his hand on the ignition key, his eyes trying to focus on the sign reading: PARKING FOR DR. ROYAL'S PATIENTS ONLY. OTHER VEHICLES WILL BE TOWED, etc., each black letter ghosting against the white background.

Seven and black as the heart of Herod, the slayer of Israel's first-born sons. Seventy-plus miles from here to home and two lanes all the way. Be home, he went on to the windshield, *if I make it all, in two hours. No snow. Too cold to snow. No moon. "No moon to show us the way to go home."* He beat out the tune on the cold hard plastic of the steering wheel.

Charlie was not talking to himself. He was talking to the VW. He spent a lot of time in the VW, making the rounds for Pelvex, Inc., ObGyn supplies, covering all of Connecticut, parts of Westchester, the Berkshires and slices of Massachusetts and Rhode Island for good measure. There was time spent in the VW, not driving, just sitting as he was doing at the moment, or shuffling cards in the morning, arranging the order of his calls, or mustering his courage to get off his butt and go into the next doctor's office to make his pitch—"detail" was the trade euphemism—or just dreaming about what he'd rather be doing, which was anything but what he had to do. And time spent trying to make a decision—not an easy thing for Charlie to do.

All that time taken together—the miles of driving, the hours of sitting, of dreaming—had established a certain rapport between him and his car. They talked to each other.

Dr. Albert Royal had rules about seeing Detail men, preferring the mornings before he saw his first patients. If he had not been in surgery he'd see the Detail men then, whom he did not particularly like. The morning press of twenty or more patients in the waiting room pushed them to hurry through their spiel. The few Detail men that Dr. Royal enjoyed talking to—and Charlie was one of them—he'd see after the last patient had gone.

Dr. Royal and Charlie were on their second Old Taylor and branch water. Charlie wiggled his glass back and forth, looking for the right word in the amber swirl. "Well," he said, lifting his eyes to the oil that Dr. Royal had propped against the portable bar. "Well, it's damn good." *You bloody liar,* he thought. Smiling, he turned to the doctor. "Damned good."

Dr. Royal returned his smile. Thin pink lips stretched across the broad, square, brown and red time-bespeckled face, his tired eyes faintly blue in the white neon lights of the elaborately-furnished attic studio. Dr. Royal had taken up painting late in life. The wood paneling of the studio bore the fruit of his efforts begrudgingly. Mostly portraits, still lifes and one or two landscapes; the colors were intense, the drawing rudimentary, and composition nonexistent. Dr. Royal showed his paintings at medical conventions. He won prizes, as some of the oils bore witness, festooned as they were with blue, red or gold ribbons.

The doctor had gone for the four dozen diaphragm deal—assorted sizes—gets you one free manometer with the latest thing in cuffs—velcro! Hot dog. He had also ordered fifty of the Dr. Gorman Marital Guides. Charlie had to be nice to him. Hell, he always had to be nice whether he ordered or not. He had to be nice to all the doctors. Even when he thought them shits. "Damned good," he repeated.

Doctor Royal was not an ObGyn specialist. He wasn't a board-certified surgeon. He wasn't an internist. There were a lot of things Dr. Royal was not, besides not being a Renoir. Yet Dr. Royal had been delivering babies, repairing prolapses, removing appendixes, and treating patients for cancer, cirrhosis of the liver, and for all he, Charlie, knew, leprosy. He'd been practicing medicine for forty years in the town of Torrington. His patients were the children, grandchildren, great grandchildren of the first patients he had ever had. To all these patients he was The

Doctor—what they supposed all doctors to be. And since most of them had survived his ministrations one way or another, he was passed along to friends and relatives ad infinitum. As for those who died while in his hands...well, you can't win them all.

Charlie fell back into the deep Naugahyde wing chair. Royal's smile broadened. His teeth, Charlie noted, were still the small, irregular brown-stained teeth that had surprised him on his first call six years ago, and surprised him still. You'd think a doctor... but not Royal. Too busy.

"Well, that's a damn sight better than saying it's interesting. When anybody tells me it's interesting I know what he means. He just hasn't the nerve to say it's no good, right, Charlie? You're an artist."

Charlie took a deep drink. He held up his hand in protest. "No. No. I'm not an artist."

"You've studied art," the doctor broke in. "You told me you did some painting."

"Yes, but not any more. Hell, no. My definition of an artist is a guy who arts...haha...a man who works at it, that paints. You know what I mean?" He sat up and leaned forward. "That has to paint or draw every day. When you stop practicing medicine they will still call you 'Doctor'. 'Doctor Royal'. They call a governor 'Governor' even after he's been kicked out of office and ain't governing no more. You see? But a pianist that's stopped playing the piano, a writer who has run dry, a painter who hasn't drawn a line or painted an eyelash...none of them can be called artists. Has-beens, maybe. But not artists." Charlie sank back into his chair.

"Well, why did you stop painting, for God's sake?"

"Hey, that's a long story."

It's still the same old story, Charlie sang to the steering wheel, *because nobody's givin' and you gotta make a livin'....What is it dear old Irenee says...she puts it so well...hmmmnn. Oh, yeah. Me: Lookit, we'll make it all right. Just keep it within our means, that's all. Don't spend what we haven't got. Says she, dear old Irenee: Oh, we'll manage. You'll find a way. Me:* Charlie hammered on the wheel. *Until we do, just spend as much as I make, okay? There's the kids in college ...cliché, dear old Beetle, cliché ... .But the*

3

thing about clichés is that that's the way things are. The kids are in college and the old man is paying for their room and board, books and tuition. Geeze.

Charlie had pulled the unyielding wheel to his chest. His head hit the windshield. *And then good old Irene said . . .get this, baby, . . .he beat on the steering wheel . . ."The idea is not to spend less but to make more." Yeah, that's what she says.* Charlie guffawed. Make more. Ha! Charlie had made ten calls, plus one to the hospital where the chief surgeon had come out covered with blood to look at the speculum he was trying to sell the hospital. The blood had unnerved Charlie and he had given a pisspoor demonstration. The doctor wasn't buying, but he did take the time to tell Charlie that prostrate operations were damned messy but really little more than a tonsillectomy. *Thanks a bunch, Doc. I can hardly wait.* Charlie laughed. Of the ten calls, he had gotten in to see five doctors, Royal being the last, because Royal always took him up to the attic for a drink, and he had needed a drink. Total sales gross—$150.00 Total commission for Charlie— thirty bucks. Plus the few bucks he'd make on mileage, which was figured on Fords and not VW's. He had the edge there, though it was taking its toll on his six-foot-plus frame. He shifted on the plastic seat of the VW.

Dr. Bella Jackson. No trouble seeing her. The waiting room was empty. A black-bordered photo of Medgar Evers.

Dr. Jackson's specialty was ObGyn. As she put it, "What else could it be for a woman—a colored woman at that?"

"Well, you're just starting out," Charlie said. "I've seen it before. Pretty soon you'll have more patients than you can handle."

She smiled. She was real pretty when she smiled. Actually, she was pretty period. A smooth, young face, large eyes, nice lips... *If I could paint her, I'd use a violet ground and glaze over burnt umber with a touch of blue to cool it. If I could paint her. If I could spend the night, an hour or two...* Irene hated it when he sang. But the old VW didn't mind. He rocked himself on the wheel. Well. He wasn't about to try to con Dr. Jackson into spending any of her hard not-yet-earned money on Pelvex, Inc. items. He gave her a set of fitting rings for the diaphragm, a tube of vaginal jelly, a package of douche powder of the right ph, an order blank, and as he was leaving—so she would not see what it was while he was still there—he left her a copy of Dr. Harmon Gorman's how-to-screw book.

"Called on a new doctor in town today." Charlie wanted to get away from the arty discussion with Royal. Get his mind off it. "Pretty woman name of Jackson. She'll be relieving you of some of your load, I expect," Charlie said, wondering how Royal would react. He was always complaining about how his practice didn't leave him enough time to paint.

"Not likely, not likely." Royal got up and moved to straighten one of his paintings. "Pretty, isn't it?" he said, beaming fatly at a mishmash of blues, ochres and white balls that was supposed to be some kind of seascape.

"Yeah," Charlie said, deliberately misunderstanding. "She's pretty."

"Ha," Royal let out. "Thinking of changing your luck? Better hurry. That coon won't last six months in this town."

Geeze! Charlie banged on the steering wheel. He stamped his foot. *Goddamn it! Why didn't I tell the fat bastard off? Why why why? It's still the same old story. Charlie,* Charlie addressed himself and not the VW for the first time. *You're becoming a fink. A yellow shit. But then most of the $150 came from Royal that day. Yeah, but many a day I've spent on the picket lines for Willie McGee, for Medgar Evers, James Meredith, the Martinsville Seven. Geeze! Hell, didn't I root for Jackie Robinson? Robeson's my number one hero. And I sit there, drink his booze..."That Coon!"* *Geeze!* Charlie gripped the wheel, squeezed his eyes tightly shut. A tear ran down his cheek. "Geeze, is this me?" he asked the Beetle.

Dr. Perlemutter was another one. Being Jewish, for some reason Charlie could not understand, Perlemutter never failed to have at least one Jewish joke to tell each time Charlie called. Perlemutter had taken the foam rubber pelvic model that Pelvex, Inc. had designed and manufactured for the purpose of demonstrating its various products out of Charlie's hand along with the cervical dilator he was demonstrating. "This reminds me of a patient of mine."

Charlie could tell from the sly grin on his rosy, round, glistening face that one of his gags was on its way. Charlie braced himself, prepared to laugh at the right moment. "This patient, you understand, she's Jewish, no longer a spring chicken, has read somewhere about something called a Pap smear. Are you listening?" Charlie smiled and nodded. "So she says to me, 'Dr. Perlemutter, so what is a Pap smear that every woman my age should have one? There is such a thing? A Pap? We have Paps?' "

They both laughed, Charlie hoping that was the end of the joke. Not too bad. But his hopes were dashed as Perlemutter pulled himself together to go on. "So I explained to her about the Greek, Dr. Papanicolaou, George Nicholas" (not letting Charlie or himself forget that he was straight A's upper ten, kindergarten through Med School—horray!) "cervical smear, etc., cancer check-up, you know the procedure." Charlie nodded. "'Mrs. Miller,' I tell her, 'it might be a good idea to do that now as long as you are here.' Sitting there where you are sitting, she clamps her knees together and screeches, 'It's an office procedure?' 'No, no. In the examination room. Mary will set you up, it won't take a minute.' Mrs. Miller stands up, she says, 'No, thank you, Dr. Perlemutter. Not today. Some other time.' Well, I'm not one to push it, right, Charlie? I tell her to see Mrs. Smith to set up an appointment. So listen to this, Charlie. She comes in today and Mary preps her. She's in the stirrups. I'm about to insert the speculum when Mrs. Miller pops up . . .this will kill you, Charlie . . . .Charlie braced himself. " . . .'See, Dr. Perlemutter,' she beams, 'nothing to smear. I spent all week washing and scrubbing. So clean you could eat off it . . .'"

Perlemutter fell back in his padded swivel chair but managed to keep his eyes on Charlie to make sure he got it. Charlie roared. Hahahaha. What the hell, it turned out to be a sale of the dilator and a couple of other items. There was more to selling than just a line.

What a day! Charlie was asking the VW for sympathy. *What a day!*

There was Dr. Collins in his gull wing Mercedes 380 who

bought everything Charlie ever showed him. And never used. So that unless Charlie came up with a new item there was no sale. The booklets were new. Collins had been fascinated by the line drawings depicting a modest sixteen how-to positions. "I'm glad these are detachable," he said. "I won't give them to my older patients. Hell, they'd all wind up at the chiropractor's".

Dr. Feldstein, who was surely cracking up, but not from laughter. Dr. Feldstein's office was invariably jammed with women and kids. Feldstein had two nurses and a receptionist. He had moved his office as far out of town as he possibly could go and still be within emergency time to the hospital. "I've raised my fees," he cried, "I've moved away from where they live. But they keep coming. They keep coming. I can't get rid of them." If his hands had not been busy with the new fertility kit Charlie was showing him, he would be wringing them. "The more I charge," he cackled, a wild look in his eyes, "the tougher I make it for them to get to me, the more desirable I become." He threw the plastic device back to Charlie. "No, no. Thank god for the infertile ones. Who needs more babies? I send them to Collins... anyone. Not me."

"Ah," Charlie dared, "why don't you refer some of your patients to Dr. Jackson?"

"Who? Oh. The Negress." Charlie winced. "Maybe I'll do just that. She ought to be able to handle the fifty-nine varieties of vaginitis that seem to be endemic to these parts."

"Well," Charlie tried a little heartiness, "she ought to be able to do more than that, Doctor. The sheepskin reads 'Johns Hopkins'."

"What?" Feldstein was surprised. "I thought she was one of those Howard products."

"Nope. Saw it in the office with my own eyes. Matter of fact, I was surprised too. I didn't know any Negroes, let alone female Negroes, were ever admitted," Charlie said, emphasizing the word 'Negro'.

"It's a thought," Feldstein came to his feet in a dismissal. "But I doubt if any of those cows out there would go to a colored doctor—a woman at that." He had shown Charlie to the door.

No sale. Charlie addressed the vacant passenger seat, patting the cold plastic seat. *Couldn't sell him a Pelvex product and couldn't sell him on Dr. Jackson.* Dr. Feldstein was headed for a crack-up, of that Charlie was sure. *He's gonna be run over and trampled to death by all them cows, yes sir, and you know what? He doesn't even know that he's going to love it when it happens.* Charlie smoothed the plastic...it was cold to his touch; grey, though he could not see the color in the dark. *The hides of flayed Jews, fresh from Auschwitz and Berchtesgaden.*

Charlie had had a hard time talking to the doctor about a Pelvex superior speculum, an important part of the demonstration being the insertion of the tri-bladed instrument into the foam rubber model. Then the retraction and locking in place, thus affording a panoramic view of the vaginal rugae, the cervix, the cervical os—all in technicolor—and so forth. He described the action as he went through the procedure. But Dr. Stadt remained standing, looking out the window, his back to Charlie.

"Would you like to try it, Doctor?" Charlie offered the pelvic model and the speculum to the doctor's back.

"Is that your car out there?" Charlie noted the slight accent.

"Which one, the VW?" Charlie said to his back. "The baby-blue VW, that's mine."

He expected the doctor to say something like how do you like it, how does a big galoot like you fold into it, how many miles does it get to the gallon. All the stuff he'd heard before.

"Chaikin," the doctor said, looking at Charlie's calling card as he turned around, walked to his desk and sat down. His soft brown eyes fixed on Charlie's soft brown eyes, his lean blue-jowled face seemed made of stone, his lips barely moved.

He said—Charlie smoothed the passenger seat with one hand, the other on the wheel of the VW—*"Do you know what the upholstery cover on Volkswagons is made of?" Geeze! Made me sick to my stomach. Apologue, of course. Of course. The way I look at it, Dr. Stadt, this is the People's car—volks wagon,* he explained unneccessarily, the hard face with the soft eyes haunting him. *Adolph Hitler promised every good German in the thousand-year Reich a car. This promise kept them going. Like Hoover, you know about Herbert Hoover, Dr. Stadt, our Depression president of the thirties. A chicken in every pot, two cars in every garage? Huh, well anyway...of course in different directions, but in the end Hoover*

8

*did not make chickens or cars and Hitler got it up the pazoola and I
was there helping to shove it. So I figure it's still a people's car, only
we are the people who get them, see?*

Charlie had said none of that to the doctor, because when the
doctor had extended his arm to hand the Pelvex calling card back
to him, Charlie had seen the blue numbers tattooed on his
exposed wrist. Charlie had packed away the model and the speculum. Had taken his leave without a word. Charlie had headed for
Dr. Royal. Dr. Royal and Old Taylor. Stadt had been no sale.

Charlie did not tell Dr. Royal why he had given up painting.
To do that—honestly, that is—would have meant explaining
how come he had moved from the City to the suburbs; from the
picket lines to the PTA meetings; from a save-the-world philosophy to one of save-your-ass. But that was all on the outside.
Inside, Charlie was the same as he had been for all his adult
life—against war, against racism, against chauvinism of any sort,
and so on, and quite willing, as he often had back in the old days,
to put his life and/or livelihood on the line where and when it was
called for. *Trouble is, can't be one thing inside and act totally
contrariwise in the face of the growing orneriness that abounds.
Sooner or later something has to give. All those principles are going
to be . . .going? . . .maybe half gone by now . . .eroded. Yes.*

Charlie sat sober and stunned, staring blankly at the peeling
white paint, every familiar bare spot revealed in the glare of the
VW's headlights, the overhead doors of the Chaikin's garage. It
took him some time to accept the fact that he was not parked at
Dr. Royal's. He was in his own driveway, seventy-six miles
more-or-less south of Torrington, and he hadn't the foggiest
notion of how he had come to be where he was. Becoming
conscious of the gurgling engine, he reached for the ignition
switch. As he did so, he caught sight of his watch. Eight. He
brought the watch to his ear. Tickticktick. He looked closer. The
second hand swept around.

Charlie switched off the motor and the lights and set the hand
brake. He performed the necessary acrobatics getting out of the
car, slamming the door behind so that the taut canvas of the sun
roof momentarily bulged. There was a light in the kitchen.
Charlie stood staring at it, trying desperately to remember some
thing about the trip.

9

What had happened to Waterbury, Meriden, Shelton, the Merrit Parkway, Bridgeport? He shivered. He was sweating, shivering, and scared. He had been there and now, sixty minutes later, he was here and there was nothing in between.

The VW crackled and snapped as it settled down. Charlie inhaled the stench of overheated rubber and hot oil. Trembling and shaking his head in disbelief, he turned to the house.

Though it was only eight, Irene was where he had become accustomed to finding her—in bed, in the darkened bedroom that smelled vaguely of powders, perfumes and Ben Gay. "Don't turn on the light. I have a headache." Hardly news to Charlie.

"I'm leaving early in the morning," Charlie said, "so I have to tell you this now. I'm going to New York."

"Mmmmm," Irene indicated reception of this information.

"I don't know when I'll get back. Not for a couple of days, anyhow." Irene's silence posed a question. Something more had to be said. Charlie said it.

"I'm quitting the job." He hurried on. "I'll find something to do in New York."

"Why?" Irene sat up.

"Why?" Charlie repeated. Why, would anyone know why? Would she if he said, "I just covered seventy-six miles in one hour, should have taken closer to two, and I don't remember one bloody mile of the entire trip"?...The photo of Medgar Evers...

"Listen, Irene," he said. "I have to get back to the city, where the action is." That didn't sound like much. But all he could think of to say further was, "I have to get back."

TAKE CARE OF MY CAT
Boyce Tenery

Arnold Magruder was his name—Arnold because of parental whim, Magruder because of a lineage which decreed a rugged and bony frame. He liked neither his name nor his person nor, indeed, his fellow man. He did not seek the glances of women or offer them his. Taciturn and glowering, he was admirably cast in the role of Efficient Materials Manager, a position requiring intense rapport with the computer and little with his peers.

He was brutishly graceless, a man with gray eyes bulging behind fish-bowl lenses and a bulbous, balding head, forced by the restraints of poor vision to bob in a predatory manner. He resembled a praying mantis more than anything.

He spoke in rags and patches of syntax, addressing man and computer alike in unadorned cores of thought. I am inclined to be garrulous and have no idea why he sought, or even tolerated, me, who worked in Personnel. But he often accompanied me to a nearby bar after work. He drank, but never heavily, and complained bitterly about his lot.

"Why, John?" His voice rumbled deep inside his bitterness.

"Why what? Explain, my friend."

"Work—eat—why? You—why?"

"Why do I work? Companionship. Money. The pleasure of living. The same reasons, I suspect, that sustain you—all of us. Don't you have other friends?"

"You." He drank deeply. "Cat."

"You have a cat?"

"Crippled. Found her."

"What's her name?"

"Cat."

"And that's all? No family?"

"Brother. Sister." Magruder sighed. "Helen. Like cat—crippled." Then a scowl plowed through his face. "Brother?

11

Richard. Hah! King Richard!" He fell silent, breathing heavily.

"But they *do* come by?" I prompted. "Helen? Christmas. Can't walk—hurts. Richard? First Tuesdays. Wife—Musette. Duty. Kiss like dry sand." His voice was like dry sand, but a strange light kindled in his eyes. "One day—one day!"

One day—what? In the malevolence of his tone, the cadence of his broken phrases, lay a chilling threat. Obviously, Richard, in his monthly visits, found no benign response in Magruder. But what might happen "one day" was left unsaid, and Magruder ordered a rare second beer, as though to purge Richard from his thoughts. He drank it in silence and stood to leave.

"The mind, John...." He tapped his forehead. "The mind—anything."

Increasingly the mind obsesses him. Our table in the tavern became a podium from which he lectured on the computer mind, limited in its accomplishment only by the mastery of its programmer.

"*Better* than computer," he argued. "Computer follows—mind leads."

I'd long since quit trying to unravel his tortured thesis. "Could you give me an example?"

He held his mug before him, so agitated that he slopped beer down its side. "This is reality. Mind creates reality. Change mind—change reality. No mug. You see?"

"I see the mug. Neither you nor I can change its reality."

Swinging his arm violently, he shattered the mug on the table. "Reality changes. Always changes. You'll see. You'll see."

"I see in my files that your vacation starts next week. That's a reality we can agree on, I think."

He smiled. "Change subject?" His lips worked in and out. "Need favor." He waited as though expecting a refusal.

"Name it."

"Feed cat."

"Of course." You'll have to show me—I assume you have a schedule of sorts?"

Magruder stood. "Come with me."

His house was immaculate and small, nevertheless graceful, with scrubbed white walls and flowing green trim, the garden and lawn in loosely-held restraint. A plump orange and white cat with one leg oddly askew purred on the cocoa mat at the door. It waited patiently, following Magruder with its yellow eyes, then skinned through the door ahead of us as it opened.

A hall with a bathroom at the end divided the house. One side was a single large room serving as kitchen, dining and living room, which betrayed nothing of his habits except by the absence of trinkets and opened books—an impartial and secretive cleanliness. His life, I felt, lay behind the four closed doors on the other side—or in Cat, now pacing back and forth—step, step, dip.

Magruder smiled at the creature and took from a cabinet two bowls and a can. He filled one bowl with water and placed it carefully on the floor, wiping up a few spilled drops. Opening the can, he spooned its contents into the other bowl, which he placed beside the first. The cat purred.

"Don't be deceived," he said. "Cat's gratitude connects to stomach."

Cat attended to, he opened an invisible trap door in one corner of the kitchen, descending into a small cellar to retrieve a bottle of wine. He motioned me to the table, got two wine glasses from another cabinet, and sat.

"That's all?" I asked.

"At night—let in. Morning—let out."

"She requires very little."

Magruder splayed his hands. "Throw cans away—wash bowls. Too much?"

"Of course not."

"Need key." He placed an old-fashioned house key on the table.

"My vacation starts at the end of yours. I won't be able to return it immediately."

"You keep it." Magruder hesitated, grimacing. "May need it."

He took the wine glasses to the sink and washed them, indicating that the conversation had ended.

For three weeks I came each morning to let the cat out, each evening to feed her. I washed the bowls and dusted the furniture, but I respected the closed doors. The first Tuesday morning I noted, but did not touch, the envelope addressed to Helen in Magruder's angular printing. Tuesday evening it was gone. Other than that, nothing changed. Cat purred her thanks from the depths of her stomach, and the time passed.

I took my own vacation and returned in three weeks to find the office changed: a strange face sat at Magruder's desk. I learned that he had not returned to work following his vacation. I called his home without an answer and, flipping through his file, found Richard's number. He was at work, of course, but his wife, Musette, answered in a tired voice, explaining, insisting, that Arnold was quite well when she last saw him.

"No," she said, when pressed, "he was not in when we called, but I never pry into his affairs. He left an envelope for Helen, which Richard delivered."

I did not have Helen's number. I should have asked Musette for it, but found it too much an effort to call her back and lost myself in the pile-up work. I finally turned to my private correspondence. The third envelope that surfaced was typed, marked PERSONAL. Inside the envelope I found a key, but no letter. Thinking it might be a promotional gimmick, I slipped the key in my pocket and forgot it.

After a hectic day I went to my usual bar, where Magruder's absence only deepened my concern. I decided to go by his home.

Arriving, I knocked, then called. I shuffled about nervously, reluctant to enter without invitation, but unwilling to walk away. I finally unlocked the door and entered. Cat, emaciated and ragged, lapped water from a bowl in the sink. She looked at me wildly, growled, and struggled through a narrow slot at the bottom of the partially opened window over the sink. On the floor I counted nine cans of cat food, obviously there for some time as their odor had ripened to a pervading stench. Over the furnishings a film of dust hid the one-time polish.

I opened the trap door in the kitchen, descended a short ladder, and turned on the light. There were no hiding places in the cellar—he was not there. That left the four unopened doors. I had selected one, when a telephone rang in another—the one nearest the front door. I opened that one, surprised to find nothing inside but a chair, a small circular table, and the ringing telephone. I answered it.

14

My "Hello" produced a deep sigh of relief from the caller, but
it was followed immediately by a hesitant question.

"You're . . .not Arnold?"

"No. I dropped by after work when he was not at the office. I'm
John Brownlee."

"Oh . . . He's spoken of you. This is Helen."

"His sister?"

"Yes." I sensed her sudden excitement. I could visualize her
distraught face, feel her growing fear. "Arnold hasn't been in
for—oh, my God!—six weeks, Mr. Brownlee. I know something
has happened to him. Does anything look—you know—is there
evidence of any trouble? Things disarranged—a robbery?"

"No. Of course I haven't looked around yet. Dust. Cat food.
The place looks deserted. You've called every day?"

"Oh, more often. Sometimes twice—three times—I can't say
exactly."

"You haven't come over?"

"It's somewhat difficult for me. But . . .could you please help
me?"

I agreed, of course, and took her number. I then went
through the house methodically. Nothing was out of place or
incongruous, except the cat food and the bowl in the sink, with
water dripping slowly from the faucet, but everywhere was the
film of dust which Arnold would never have tolerated. In one
room I found rows of display cases filled with rocks and crystals, each with a neatly-typed card which I did not take time to
read. There was the telephone room, and Arnold's bedroom,
sparsely furnished.

The final room contained a file cabinet, a desk and chair, and a
typewriter which, among all the meager appointments of his
house, was free of dust. Clearly printed in the dust on the file
cabinets were fingerprints.

The file cabinet! I remembered the key, and dug in my pocket
for it. It worked. I opened the bottom drawer first, from habit—
that's where I always file matters of importance. This one contained folders relating to the mineral collection—nothing else.
In the middle drawer I found manuscripts. I glanced through
them, beginning to read compulsively. They were stories,
strange and haunting fantasies. Hardly what I would have ex-

pected from him, but they bore his by-line, and he would be above plagiarism. I forced myself to go to the next drawer, which held more stories.

The top drawer was different. Conspicuously askew in the front was a manilla envelope bearing my name in large block letters. I took it and sat at the desk to open it.

The whisper of a sharp, expectant breath stopped me in the act of removing a thin sheaf of papers. I rose and stepped to the door. I looked up and down the hall, and crossed it to look in the large room; but I saw nothing unusual, and returned to the typewriter room.

The first sheet in the folder contained but one sentence: "Please take this home and read it." I swallowed an overpowering curiosity and did as I was asked. That night, I read in the quiet of my study.

My alienation from society is not a thing of my choosing, good friend, but one to which I have been driven by a malignancy that has stalked my life for sixteen years. I was once in love, and I would return from evenings in the arms of my beloved to rush to Helen's room, demanding that she assure me I had said the right things. I would repeat the confidences of my love, to hear her say, "Yes, Arnold, you are right. She loves you."

Helen was deeply involved in my life, as you may have guessed. One day, with a sister's curiosity, she followed me—perhaps to observe, to see that I reported accurately to her, and that I was not being led to disappointment. Elisabeth, the girl, had prepared a picnic basket and we climbed the slopes of a small mountain to a level meadow near its summit.

We were scarcely seated when Elisabeth raised a finger to her lips. "I hear something," she said. "Someone has followed us."

I heard nothing, but rashly, as a young man too often is, I dislodged a large boulder with my foot. "I'll sweep them from our mountain," I boasted.

The loosened rock gathered an avalanche, roaring down the slope. It was then I heard an agonized scream. I was horrified, for I recognized Helen's voice. I rushed down the incline, sliding and tumbling, my terror growing as I seemed unable to move. At last I reached Helen, half buried in loose rocks and sand. Her legs were cut and broken, crushed, I thought, to a pulp. She moaned softly, unable to move. Her back was oddly twisted, and I was afraid to move her. I sat with Helen, reassuring her, holding her hand, while Elisabeth went for help.

Needless to say, Helen lived, but she was seriously crippled. She has never recovered.

She has never blamed me—I am my own accuser. I, and Richard, who gloats, I think, over reminding me. I give Helen my share of our inheritance so that she will not be forced to add penury to her disability; but Richard, who controls its disbursement, will not permit me to sign over my share. No. He must come, month after month, to repeat his act of accusation, to renew my contrition with each check I endorse.

No, Helen has never blamed me. She visits me each Christmas, and would more often, but I know she must suffer from so extended an outing. I do not visit her, fearing, I think, to see the pain exacted by the slightest task. She never fails to comment on the neatness of my house. I see her, with her disability, unable to keep her own place in a way she would approve of and I would not subject her to shame by discovering it in disarray. I respect her pride and content myself with our telephone calls.

Perversely, I blamed Elisabeth for the accident, and cut her out of my life. This rankling condemnation of an innocent person brewed a venom in my blood, turning me to hate all mankind, as though humanity had joined in a conspiracy to destroy Helen. I withdrew from all association, as you well know, discovering too late that my solitude neither benefited Helen nor atoned for my thoughtless act. When I finally wanted companionship I could not truly unlock my cell. My hatred had become an obsession centered around Richard.

I set myself in all the paths of hate and loneliness. Pity—self pity—constrained from growing, grew inward. "I want no one to call" became "No one ever calls." Even there the insidious growth did not cease. Like a punished child I devised a fantasy: if they should come, they would be sorry if I were no longer here. Then they would repent. They would know how cruelly they had treated me, all those who never called.

Above all, my hatred demanded that Richard suffer; but like a child, I wanted to see his suffering. Whoever says "They'll be sorry when I die," always imagines himself observing that sorrow. Thus I planned my vengeance.

When Richard called the first Tuesday of your vacation I hid in the cellar and let him search the house, calling me. Good, I thought. He is worried. He feels guilt. His first Tuesdays would become his own act of penance.

He did come and roam my empty house while I crouched in gloating, miserable happness in the cellar. The telephone rang—

Helen. How I longed to answer. But I could not release my secret without releasing Richard from his suffering.

I fed Cat, and in my solitude I thought again of the power of the mind—of how I could by a force of will become invisible, if that became my reality. Then I could not only listen to Richard's fruitless searching: I could watch it. I concentrated on this for hours, alone.

I knew I had gone too far a week ago. I had waited for the dark of a moonless night, intending to water my garden without disclosing myself. I reached for the doorknob. My hand passed through it, without resistance! The walls had lost their substance—were shadows, no more. Wildly, I rushed about the house. I ran to the telephone. It, too, was a ghost. That night I went to bed and lay awake, stroking the blanket, turning the pillow, running my hand over Cat's soft fur, fearful that these things, too, would dissolve before my touch. I awoke late. The sun streamed in my window, and for the length of a breath I knew that I had only dreamed. I jumped from the bed to wind the clock. I touched a shadow.

My house has become a mirage, a ghost of walls around the shadows of my meager possessions. Only in my study, my world of unreality, does reality remain. I can open my files, touch the smooth sheets of paper, roll them into my typewriter. I can write and must do so quickly while I can. I have placed a key to my file cabinet in an envelope and slid it under the door. I can only hope the postman takes it. I cannot leave the drawers unlocked, for even now, I will not let Richard know.

I have unwittingly abandoned Helen. You must see that Richard transfers my annuity to her, that she does not again suffer through me. Please do as I ask, I can only watch. In this strange full void I need no food—but please take care of my cat.

I fed his cat the following day, then went into the study. I sat at his typewriter, ran my hands over it, the last thing he'd been able to touch. I fed a sheet of paper into it. While I watched, the type bars came to life, straining, trembling, falling back without striking a mark. Harder! harder! I willed them, reaching out to touch the keyboard. I heard a sigh—a wind in the room—and my fingers followed the keys, striking hard and clear.

Not quite a line. They stopped, tingling as though they'd been asleep. I looked.

"Please don't leave me alone."

Richard would not consent to a transfer.

"If he's dead, there's no body," he said. "It'll be seven years before he can be declared dead."

"And you'll do nothing?"

"Nothing. Without proof, nothing."

I could not expect Helen to believe the truth, and explained only that Arnold had written he must leave. She was standing at a window, looking as small and slender as a child. Her arms were raised to her head. She turned to me, and loosed her long, black hair.

"I realize there's much you aren't saying, but is he all right? Can you assure me of that?"

"Yes. Are you well?"

She smiled. "My 'disability'?"

"Arnold said it was quite painful."

She laughed. "Not really. I rarely notice."

"He said that was why you only visited him on Christmas."

"I only visited him on Christmas because I upset him. He'd spend weeks afterwards blaming himself all over again. It was kinder to him that he think me unable."

I went to Richard with the request that he rent me Arnold's house.

"That's between you and Arnold," he said. "It's nothing to me."

Yet, I was not to leave Arnold alone.

I found a perfect solution. I live there now, with Helen—Helen Brownlee now. I never see her disability, it has disappeared or perhaps was never reality. I no longer know. Some day I must explain about Arnold, but for now, she seems quite happy, and speaks of him as though he were present.

The cat left the day Helen moved in.

LOVE AND WORK:
WORK AND LOVE
Elizabeth Davis

Long shadows stretched themselves across the still garden.
The evening had set in. Shadows stretched everywhere, through
the grass, up the rock wall, into the house. Nightfall. The garden
still as ever. Only a snake slipping through the twilight grass.

"Do you want a cup of tea?" she asked.

"No. The brandy tastes good." Tom reached his arm across
her. "Don't get up. Not yet." He was smiling, his sweet know-it-
all smile.

V. lay back down and pushed her feet deeper into the warm
afghan. She and Tom lay on the rumpled bed, he with a cigarette
in his hand, she trying to cover herself, though the room was not
cold. Every now and then they spoke. But mostly V. listened to
the sounds in the garden and watched Tom.

"Can we go through it one more time?" she asked slowly. She
hated to break the mood but something inside her begged for
clarity. "I've thought about it some more. I think I can pinpoint
our differences this time."

Tom turned on his side and looked at her. His face was shad-
owed, his back to the twilight window. He patted her head, then
pushed back a strand of hair from her face. Like a father with his
child.

"Go ahead," he said.

V. drew in her breath. "It all comes down to this, Tom. You
and I are different. We have different philosophies about life. For
you, Love is everything—first, last and always—the reason for
being. But if I were to be honest, with you and with myself, I
would admit that, although love is wonderful, it's not everything.
Given a choice, I would have to say that between Love and Work,
Work is more important. Work defines who we are!"

"You don't love me. Is that what you're trying to tell me?"

"Please, Tom, don't joke. If we don't clear this up, it'll keep coming back. All I'm saying is that I love my work. I have to work. I have to paint every day. It's who I am." She paused to remove his hand from her head. She knew he wasn't taking her seriously. They'd had this conversation before. Sometimes he listened and seemed to understand; other times, like now, he simply let her talk herself out. She had told him over and over that Love wasn't enough for her, but he acted as if it should be. When he came to see her, Love took over, she gave in. But she couldn't do this forever. She needed rest, she needed to be away from him at times. She needed to be able to work.

They were always at odds like this, always in disparate moods. Except when they made love.

V. now reached up and turned on the small reading lamp to the left of the bed. It shed a pale yellow light on Tom's smooth, round face, on his thick brown hair, on the softer tones of his broad chest and stomach. A tall, well-built man in his late twenties, Tom was younger than V. by six years, but V. had decided that it was not their age difference so much as their approach to life that made her anxious. It had come to the point where every day was a battle. She needed Love and Work, while Tom . . . Tom needed only Love.

V. started again to rise. "I don't think you'll ever understand," she said. She stopped at the end of the bed and gathered the blue afghan around her, then stood up.

"Come here, Babe. What are you getting so upset about?" Tom stared at her in a sleepy, befuddled way. He reached out his hand.

"You know, you laugh at Mr. and Mrs. Bell," V. suddenly said, "but if you stop and think about it, they have more than we have. They have true Love. This isn't true Love."

"Where do you get all these definitions? What is it with you? Why isn't what we have enough?" Tom rose up on one elbow. "And who was talking about the Bells? They've been married for 45 years." He waited. "You want to get married, is that it?"

V. felt her heart begin to pound. "No, I don't want to get married. But I don't want you coming into my house like this and taking over either. You come here, we make love, you leave. I have to pick up all the pieces. It would be different if you worked.

21

But all you do is go home and sleep, or read. You won't ever get a job, Tom." Now V. walked to the door of the room and glared back at him. "You can't work. You're one of those 'Walking Wounded'!"

Tom sat up, his eyes glazed. He sat with his legs over the edge of the bed and reached out for his pack of cigarettes. "I don't understand you," he said, not looking at her, and shaking his head. "I've told you before, I want to be your lover, but don't count on me to be your breadwinner. That's just not me."

"Who wants your damn money?" V. shouted. She wanted to throw something at him. Damn him, so complacent. Sitting there on the side of the bed. Lighting another cigarette.

She turned and left the room.

As she walked through the house, V. did not turn on the lights. She preferred the dusky gray of half-light. In the kitchen she put on the water, then sat down at the kitchen table and looked out. The garden was deserted, the light vanished. Patches of fog gathered against the back of the house, pressing at the windows and doors like children waiting to be let in. V. listened. She could hear a dove cooing, high up, in one of the shrouded trees.

V. waited for the pounding in her chest to stop. She pulled herself tighter into the knitted blanket, ignoring the tingling of wool on her bare skin. When the kettle began to whistle, she made a cup of strong black tea, then settled into the chair by the window again. Tom was partly right. At the beginning, it had been enough. Love was enough. He had brought a single red rose the first night he had come up. And he continued to bring one, all through the fall, the winter and into the spring. But as the summer came on, the roses had stopped. The symbol had worn thin. But not his insistence. If anything, it had grown, expanded, stretched into a fuller intensity, until now, when she opened the door to him, it seemed he would enter her house and demolish her.

Calmer, V. thought of Mr. and Mrs. Bell, the old couple Tom lived with. He occupied the back of their house, rent-free, in exchange for helping Mr. Bell with the fences and gutters and the heavy work in the large garden. V. also suspected they liked his company and, perhaps, they felt he protected them too. Whenever V. went by to see Tom, Mr. Bell would be out in the garden, even on the rainiest of days. He would slowly walk to the gate, hand outstretched to her, looking like a frail black spider in his dark padded vest, long thin arms, dark-skinned face. "I'm getting ready to help Mrs. Bell," he would say, smiling at V. and wiping the moisture from his eyes with a folded handkerchief. "She's out in the potting shed again." He'd lean back his head and laugh. V. would take his thin, dry hand and walk to the house with him, knowing that Mrs. Bell never left her bed now, knowing that "the potting shed" was only Mr. Bell's sad joke.

Tom was rearranging the sheets and pillows when V. returned. He was still undressed. The sight of his back sent a shiver through V. She gazed at the curve of his wide shoulders and slim hips. She was thinking about his kindness to the Bells, his kindness also to her. He hardly ever got angry with her.

"I'm sorry," she said softly. "You're not a 'Walking Wounded.'"

"If you really meant it," he said, turning to face her, "you'd call it off, right?" He smiled, then picking up his red plaid shirt from the floor, began to dress, buttoning his shirt in an odd way, from the bottom up. V. went to the dresser and switched on a second light. She watched him, thinking how much she liked his full, almost pouting lips, his round blue-gray eyes. He was tame and gentle. In time, he would resemble Mr. Bell. Whether he worked or not was his problem, not hers. V. was surprised by her own rationality.

With his clothes on, Tom came and stood in front of her. "It's going to be all right, it really is, V." He reached out his hand and touched her bare shoulder. He smiled. "Do you want to get some sleep? Or are you going back to work on your painting?" He smiled again and gazed at her, waiting. Then he turned and began to lead her to the bed. V. felt her determination melt, her body relax. Suddenly she could think of nothing but the feel of his body on hers.

V. lay on the bed and watched Tom remove his clothes. He settled down next to her and gathered her in his arms. Again he stroked her shoulders and arms, as he had done earlier in the day, and again he bent to kiss her lips, then her face, then her neck, slowly, with strong but gentle strokes on her side, her shoulders, her back. V. felt herself stretching, stretching, until her body seemed the length of the bed. He moved on top of her and she held him tightly with her legs and drew herself up, tighter, closer, pulling him in to her with all her strength. She would pull him inside of her, always, closer, deeper, inside. She felt her heart pounding, a pounding in her ears, then a rise, and short, fast contractions, her own moans, wanting to let go. But he went on, ignoring her, pushing deeper into her, insisting that she go further, moving on top of her at the same steady pace, pushing in and out in a tireless rhythm, until finally the lower half of her body seemed to fold like the petals of a night-closing flower. She was crying his name, smiling and crying and happy.

She opened her eyes and looked up at him. She noticed for the first time how he held back. He seemed to be working on her, watching her face, uninvolved and remote. It was only after her cries had ceased that he grabbed her up in his arms, drew in his breath, and shuddered, his mouth forming the familiar "O", his eyes closing against the release of feeling.

For a time, they lay side by side, her cheek resting on his chest. She could smell his hot skin. She tried to sleep but when she closed her eyes, she saw the image of a woman standing naked in front of a blank canvas. The woman held in her hand a silver-pointed arrow and was jabbing the arrow into her right side. Blood streamed from the prodded wound, down her leg, into a pool of red at her feet. V. was frightened by the image but she could not push it away. She watched the woman with fascination and fear.

She waited, a half hour, perhaps more. Then turning on her side, she nudged him. "Wake up, Tom. I want you to leave."

"What?"

"I have to work. Now. Please. I want you to go home."

"I will. I'll go later. Let me sleep." He rolled over, his back to her. V. remembered how hard he had worked, bending his body over hers.

"Wake up," she said again. "It's only eight o'clock. You can be home, in your own bed, by 8:30."

Tom turned his head and stared at her. His face looked swollen with anger. "This is it, Babe. This is the last time. There's no going back, not now." His eyes looked threatening.

V. was silent. She was thinking how common the name "Babe"

sounded to her. Her insides felt like cold silver. She would not go back.

She waited until he had begun to climb out of bed before she got up, took a robe from the back of door, and swiftly left the room.

V. tiptoed through the darkened house to her studio where she flicked on the light over her easel. All around her visceral reds, blazing yellows, killing greens leapt into view. Her paintings warmed her. They *were* her. One, a large canvas, showed two voluptuous roses, screaming in their deep reds, intertwined in a crown of spikes. Another, a sunny field of golden wheat; in the center, the sleek back of a crouching panther. The painting on the easel was of a country scene, a mailbox painted over with flowers and with the words "Love" and "Peace." Inside lay a fat gray cobra, tightly-coiled and ready to strike.

V. set a new canvas onto the ledge. She began to sketch the bleeding woman, then the arrow. Through the darkened rooms, she heard the latch click shut, then a hush settle on the house. I'll make this a wing, she suddenly decided, and she began to change the coarse line of the arrow into a beautiful, triumphant pennon. Yet as she applied the paint, the image of the arrow returned, again and again, until she was forcing herself to paint the feathery lines of the wing over it. Outside in the garden the moon rose, casting white streaks across the ground. Silver glistened on the damp grass, yet because of the tall trees, the house continued to lie in shadow.

ONE DRIED SPIDER,
THREE CAT WHISKERS
Kathryn Winter

Tonight will be a full moon, the first since Whitsunday. Tonight I must do it.

At supper I'm quiet, I can hardly eat. Aunt Lena feels my forehead. I smile and force down another spoonful of cabbage noodles. Aunt Lena musn't worry. If she does, she will come to my room at night and find an empty bed!

Tomorrow evening Pavel comes home. My heart beats faster at the thought. At this time tomorrow we'll all be sitting at the table and I will feel Pavel's eyes on my face. He'll be looking at me the way he sometimes looks at Anka when he thinks no one's watching. No wonder. Anka is seventeen, with blond hair and rosy cheeks, and on Sundays, when she puts on her embroidered Slovak costume, she's got everyone gaping at her. But tomorrow Pavel won't have eyes for Anka. Pavel will look at me and he will fall in love with me.

I help Anka with the dinner dishes. My hands are trembling. Another hour before Aunt Lena sends me to bed, then two more before I leave. How do I stay awake?

Raisins! Just the thing to get some tongue-tied imp to talk. I'll take a pocketful. And Pavel's picture. At that I can gaze for hours, but one glance at Pavel makes my head spin. I want him to look at me but when he does I blush, stutter, run away and hide. But tomorrow I won't hide. Tomorrow night when Pavel looks at me I will be beautiful.

It's getting dark; stars are beginning to appear. At midnight the full moon will be overhead and I know what I must do.

Aunt Lena sends me to the pantry for bread, cheese and an apple. I find the raisins and rush to my room to hide them.

In my dresser, under a pile of woolen stockings, is the box. Inside it are all the things I need for tonight with the instructions

26

on a folded piece of paper. Old Krasovka knows her business and she made certain I understood everything she said. After she tasted the third sausage I brought her she made me write down her instructions and read them back to her, from beginning to end.

"Nonsense," she muttered when I told her what I had already tried. "Silly nonsense! Do exactly as I tell you, and in the morning—"

"The morning! You mean I have to wait till morning?"

"Be quiet and listen! After the cock crows twice, but before he crows for the third time, then, *only* then must you look. Do not fall asleep," she warned me.

"But what if— "

"No *ifs*, Katarina, this is magic! If you look too soon or too late, you'll undo it!"

"All right, all right, I'll wait . . . ."

Aunt Lena calls me back into the kitchen to give me tomorrow's lunch for school. At nine o'clock she kisses me good night and sends me to bed.

I slip on my nightgown. In the mirror I see a gawky sixth grader with red hair and freckles. I hate the freckles, hate them! It's because of my freckles Pavel keeps looking at Anka, not at me. And in school it's "Freckleface, Freckleface, what's that all over your face?" "She fell asleep under the apple tree— the sparrows got her!" "Nah, those are bat droppings!" "Fly spots!" "Spider's eggs!"

The mouth twitches, the chin trembles. The mirror ripples, blurs. I wait for her to appear. She is beautiful in her green velvet gown and soft, broadbrimmed hat. Clear skin, rose colored cheeks, a slender waist. She is Katarina, the woman Pavel loves. She is I, a few years from now. "Don't go," I plead even as Freckleface, with red eyes and shiny nose pouts back at me. I stick out my tongue at her. "I won't see *you* again," I tell her. "Good riddance!"

In bed I turn on my flashlight and burrow under the bulky comforter with TRUE LOVE STORIES, a magazine I'm not allowed to read. In the dim light I scan the long columns of small print and suddenly my nose hits the page. I've been dozing! I jump out of bed, stretch, do ten deep knee bends. Another hour and a half to wait!

27

ONE DRIED SPIDER, THREE CAT WHISKERS

I try reading a love story but can't keep my mind on it. I keep glancing at the clock and I worry; will the garden gate squeak and wake Aunt Lena? Will someone from the village see me? Will I find my way in the dark? Is everything I need in the box? I take it out from the dresser and check each item against my list: one dried spider, three cat whiskers, a clove of garlic, the tail of a mouse, droppings of a bat and the ointment Krasovka gave me. For the umpteenth time I read the instructions. It's past ten o'clock. I close my eyes and think of Pavel.

I fell in love with Pavel the moment I saw him, but was too young to know it. That was two years ago, when I came to live with Aunt Lena and Uncle Theo, the widower she married. Pavel and his father came down the gravel path to meet us. "Light as a feather," he said, lifting me so high that my hair tangled with a branch of the nut tree. I plucked a leaf and rubbed it against my cheek. "Kiss Pavel," Aunt Lena prodded, "he's your new cousin." He was looking up at me, smiling, and I felt heat coloring my face and rushing down my neck. "Put me down," I shouted, wrenching off a fistful of leaves. "Down, down!" "Look at her blushing," Aunt Lena laughed. There I was, up high, for everyone to see. "It's not true," I burst into tears. "I'm n-not b-b-blushing!" Pavel lowered me gently and covered my cheeks with his palms. Smells of cigarettes and something I didn't recognize. It was then I felt it for the first time. I didn't know what it was but knew I couldn't bear feeling any more of it. I grabbed Pavel's hand, bit it, and ran.

Pavel's hands smell of green wood even after he scrubs them with a brown paste, the smell of which I hadn't recognized in the garden. He works in a sawmill far down the river and comes home only on weekends. Often, on Sundays, Pavel hides a chocolate bar under my pillow. I love chocolate. Usually I'd gulp it down in one minute wishing there was more but the bar Pavel leaves me lasts almost a week. I mark five even sections on the wrapper, one for each day I won't see him, and every evening after I brush my teeth I eat one fifth. That way, the less chocolate there is left, the happier I am.

Sunday nights I cry myself to sleep—Pavel will be gone at sunrise. If I'm lucky I wake to the bounce of his bike on the steps or to the squeaking of the garden gate. From behind the curtain I watch him adjust his knapsack, tuck his pants into his boots, mount the bike and ride down the hill. I stay at the window, blowing kisses, long after he disappears behind the poplar grove.

Mondays tulips are pale, lilac has no scent, sunflowers droop. Books are boring, games aren't any fun. People annoy me. I stay on my perch, high in the nut tree, and don't come down until dark. At night I force down a piece of Pavel's chocolate. It clogs my throat like soggy cotton and there's still such a big piece left of it, I could cry!

Tuesdays I begin to think about the past weekend. I see Pavel everywhere: sketching at his desk, oiling his bike in the hall, running up the cellar steps, sitting on a chair blowing smoke rings across the room. I think about the times Pavel looked at me and wonder if he would have looked more often had I worn a different dress. I think about what he said and what I answered and what I wish I had answered. I talk little to Pavel; mostly I grunt or shrug shoulders. Aunt Lena scolds me, but it's Pavel's fault. I'd be sitting across the table from him, telling him silently how I've missed him, how much I love him, and he'd break in with "how's school" or "did you get all your homework finished?"

In the evening, on Tuesdays, the chocolate tastes good and after the third bite there's less than half of it left. I begin to wonder what to wear to dinner on Friday.

Wednesdays I daydream. I tiptoe into Pavel's room and hug his pillow. The room smells of Pavel. I sniff his sweaters, his Sunday jacket, his ties, belts, cigarettes. In the bathroom I open his shaving cream, his after-shave lotion, the jar of brown paste he scrubs his hands with. The scents bring him so close I can hear him breathe. Arm in arm we walk along the river. I am beautiful in my green velvet gown and my soft, broadbrimmed hat. Pavel crowns me with garlands. He tells me he loves me. He takes my hand and asks me to marry him.

Bluejays, thrushes, robins—where did they all come from? On Thursday mornings, long before Anka comes to wake me, I lie on my bed listening to them. From the kitchen come smells of fresh ground coffee and of the cakes Aunt Lena is baking for the weekend. A branch of the nut tree hangs over my window. I watch it, on Thursdays, the year round: twigs encrusted in ice and when it melts, the spread of fine, green fuzz, the shape of

29

leaves as they grow and the colors they turn before they fall. On Thursdays I can jump over the brook where it's the widest; I can make rocks skip half way across the river. In class, I score the highest grades and laugh when classmates call me Freckleface.

The last piece of chocolate tastes the best. Slowly, I roll it in my mouth, crush it with my tongue, feel it melt. Was it I who a few days ago wished there was none left?

Fridays are impossible. I spill my milk, tear my shoelaces, break pencil points, stain notebooks with ink. Stairs trip me, rocks bruise my knees, doors slam on my fingers. Every few minutes I rush to the mirror to try out another hairdo, hold yet another dress up to my chin, tilt my head this way, that way, pull at my sweater at the nipples to make it stand away—oh, just a bit! But in the evening, when I am asked to set the table, I do not set a plate for Pavel.

"Another plate," Aunt Lena reminds me. "It's Friday."

"Is it?" I ask, "are you sure? The week went by so fast . . . ."

Anka is giggling. Aunt Lena bites her lip. "Put on a pretty dress," she tells me.

"Oh, must I?"

"Well, if it's too much trouble . . . ."

But I'm already at the door, eager to break into a run on the other side of it, impatient to make myself beautiful for Pavel.

Beautiful for Pavel! What time is it?

Nearly eleven! Up goes the nightgown, down the dress. I trace garlic around my lips and over my belly. Krasovka's ointment goes on my wrists and my neck. One cat whisker inside my sock, it doesn't matter which. Shoes must be worn the wrong way: right shoe on left foot. Pockets! This dress doesn't have any—I'll wear the one with the ruffle. A clove of garlic and the ointment go in one pocket, the instructions and Pavel's picture in the other. The raisins! Here, with the garlic. The rest stays inside the box. I tie a kerchief around it to make a bundle and leave.

Quietly, I turn the lock. The garden gate squeaks but no light appears in the window, no one calls after me. Do I take the back way, behind the barns? No, it'll rouse the dogs. The tavern's long been closed, no one's coming home at this hour. The night watchman, cross-eyed Fuchik! I must watch out for him! A few gulps of slivovitz, and everywhere he sees the Devil! If he spots my shadow he'll scream and take to his heels—I'll have the whole village after me! And should they catch me, what do I say? I can't tell the truth. Krasovka said if I did she'd turn me into a frog. Brrr! A mushy, slimy frog, squatting on a rock, puffing my cheeks, croaking. A muddy pond for a home, flies for dinner. I'll have webbed feet and those horrid, pop-swivel eyes! I'll never tell the truth, not if they torture me! Ouch! My shoes are torturing me; I should have practiced wearing them the wrong way. I'll never make it! Maybe I will. I'm almost at the cemetery; that shadow is the edge of the forest.

I'm hot from trying to walk fast. Hot and cold. The cold's around me like an icy border. My knees are shaking. What's there? Something's moving above that mound—holy saints, a ghost! That's a new grave, the spirit's hovering over the corpse. Dear Jesus, I'm afraid! Aunt Lena, help! What am I doing here, in the middle of the night? I'm going home. Let Pavel make eyes at Anka, I don't care! Here is his picture, in my pocket. Let me look at it, tell him, to his face: "Pavel, I don't care if you make eyes at . . . ." Oh, he's so handsome! I love you, Pavel, love you! I *am* going to the forest. Tonight is full moon, the first since Whitsunday, tonight is my chance. Krasovka's ointment will keep me from harm; she said it would and I believe her. It stinks enough to drive off a million ghosts!

Can I run? It hurts, but I do: down one hill and up another, stopping to catch my breath only when I reach the forest. I've never been in the forest at night. My teeth are chattering. The instruction sheet trembles in my hand. I hold it up to the moon and read: "Enter forest, take first turn right, follow path to St. Anton's shrine . . . ." It's a steep climb. I rest at the shrine and then look for a moonbeam between the pine branches. "Circle shrine three times. Continue walking. When path divides, turn right." I know that path, it goes to Saint Katarina's shrine. She is my patron saint, She'll help me. It's not far. It won't take longer than . . . .

"HELP! HELP!" Something's clutching the ruffle of my dress, pulling me back. Claws are digging into my thighs and ripping the backs of my knees.

"Let me go-o-o-o!" I lurch forward, stagger to the nearest tree, wrap myself around it. With my cheek pressed against the bark, I listen to my breath: it's loud enough to wake a bear! Who grabbed me, I wonder, the Devil? "Phew, phew, phew!" I make the sign of the cross. "May the earth swallow you!" Is he following me? I hold my breath: no sound of hooves—nothing stirs. Slowly, I turn my head towards the spot from which I fled. A bramble bush. But something's moving over it, what is it, cloth? Yes—a strip of cloth, caught on thorns, flutters in the breeze. My hand slides down the back of my dress to reach the ruffle and touches bare skin. Rats! What do I tell Aunt Lena?

In the shrine I kneel down to pray: "Dear Saint Katarina, please help me! Stop my teeth from chattering or they'll break— I'll look like an old, toothless baba. Is that what you want? Are you punishing me? Dear Patron Saint, forgive me. I had to steal that last sausage, I had spent all my savings! And the walnuts, too, I needed them to trade for the mouse's tail. Please don't let Aunt Lena find out. Keep her out of my room tonight and I'll never lie or steal again, I promise. I'll send all my birthday presents I get for the next five—I mean, three years, to the orphanage. And for you I'm leaving almost all of my raisins. See?"

I walk to the fallen oak and find the rock with three crosses painted on it. This is the oak that fell on the woodsman and the rock marks the spot where they found his body. His ghost haunts the woods, Krasovka said, but I was not to worry, her ointment would protect me. I am to grind a clove of garlic into the rock, then jump backward over the fallen oak. I bet some imp is lurking about, waiting for me to trip, so he can get at the raisins. May they color his teeth purple!

This part of the forest is too dense to roam in; few people do. It's dark even in daytime. I shiver. There are smells of mildew, of moldy mushrooms and rotting wood. I trip over roots, tangle in knotgrass, step into puddles ankle deep. The path disappears. I inch forward, push one branch from my eyes while another claws at my nose. Twigs hook into my hair and pull at my bundle. My whole body itches as insects scurry down my back and my nose twitches in a coil of spider's yarn. Is this the path, I wonder, or a snare? Have I strayed into forbidden grounds from which no one returns?

Suddenly, the forest opens: before me is a wide, moonlit clearing and at the far end of it gleams the Witches' Pool. There I must wait for the first stroke of midnight and do what I've been told.

I cross the clearing and crouch among the weeds. What a stench! Do witches bathe in this pool, I wonder? Do they drink from it? I open the bundle and drop the box in the water. It dips, tilts, then steadies and rests on the surface of the pool.

Black clouds rush past the moon which has turned silver and risen high in the sky. There's a cool wind—my skin feels bumpy with goose pimples. I wedge my chin between my knees and wrap my arms around them. Hoot! hoot! My heart skips a beat as I glimpse slits of green light in the laurel. Something leaps in the grass. I gasp. It's a frog. A frog? "Tell me, frog, were you a little girl once? Did Krasovka punish you, because you couldn't keep a secret?" That won't happen to me. I don't want to think about it. I'll count to one hundred, that will pass the time. One, two ... I wonder what time it is? One, two, three, four ... that tree has eyes and a mouth. An evil mouth. Five, six ... those long, spiky branches want to grab me. Seven, eight, nine, ten, eleven ... something's moving in that bush! Twelve—there, again! Thir ... someone's breathing behind my back! Holy Katarina, save me! There—it stopped! Thirteen, fourteen, fifteen, sixteen ... that cloud is like a huge head. The head of an ogre. Seventeen, eighteen, nineteen ... he's howling. Maybe his howls are heard on the other side of the moon. And there's a flock of black sheep trying to escape from the ogre. Nine—where was I, nineteen? Yes. Nineteen, twenty, twenty-one ... that box is still floating. Don't the witches want my gift?

CLANG! CLANG! The church bell! It's midnight! In a flash I'm on my knees, bending over the Witches' Pool. I cup my hands, dip them into the ... the ... is this water? It's thick like porridge and it stinks! I retch as I force it to my face. No, I can't do it! My fingers open and globs of dark mush drip back into the pool. Weeds, sleazy with slime, cling to my hands. CLANG! CLANG! I'm running out of time! I must do it. Do it now! I pinch my nose shut and with my free hand splash—no, smear the stuff over my face. "Bagic Bowers of de Dight, geep by vre ...." I gasp for air. No, this won't do, I can't hold my nose shut. I'll try again, that time won't count. "Magic Powers of the Night," splash, "keep my freckles out of sight!" Splash, smear. "Magic Powers of the Night," smear, "keep my freckles out of sight!" Splash, splash. "Magic Powers of the Night...."

The echo of the last ring still hums as I lie stretched out in the weeds, panting. My face itches with little things crawling over it, but I can't wipe it, Krasovka told me not to. I must hold it up to the moon to dry, and then the thing is done.

Done!

The thing is done, my freckles are gone! They're gone, GONE! I can't look until dawn, till after the cock crows twice, but I know they're gone, I can feel it!

"They're gone," I shout, leaping across the clearing with my arms outstretched, like wings. "My freckles are gone, I am beautiful!"

Pale clouds move across the sky but there's no howling ogre and trees don't have arms that want to seize me. Something's moving in that bush—a bird, or a field mouse rushing home, and those green lights in the laurel are the eyes of an owl. It's past midnight. It's Friday. Tonight—

"Hey there, owl," I yell, my hands cupped around my mouth, "tonight Pavel comes home! Hey there," I shout loud enough for anyone in the forest to hear, "tonight Pavel will fall in love with me!"

I dance, roll, slide down the path. I pet the rock with the three painted crosses, I skip over the fallen oak. Saint Katarina, in her shrine, is smiling at me. I blow her a kiss, then race up the hill, past the cemetery and through the village streets, to our house.

"I am beautiful, beautiful," I shout to the Whitsun moon as I throw open the garden gate, fling my arms around the nut tree and swirl round and round ....

SANCTUARY
Robert Lee Hall

I go to a movie in west Berkeley. The theater, which is in an
industrial area and shows old and foreign films, shares an ugly
concrete building with a judo school. The movie hasn't begun. I
enter an auditorium as long and almost as narrow as an alley.
Thinking I will be safe, I sit by the wall, but thuds reverberate
from next door—grunts, cries—and suddenly there is a crash, the
wall shakes, and I am knocked from my seat. Plaster sifts into my
hair; I blink white dust from my lashes.

What has happened?

The judo school is acting up.

Feeling wounded and foolish, I creep to the center aisle. The
lights dim; gradually I rearrange my soul. The movie is a love
story, French. Everyone in it, even a stubble-faced bum meander-
ing by the Seine, looks wry. I want to enjoy the sophisticated
ambience flickering before me, but the thuds next door abruptly
resume, the cries, the resounding assaults, so that the lovers in
the movie seem to be caressing in a battle zone. At first I am
outraged—I want to complain to someone, though no one else in
the theater seems to mind (is it because they, natives of Berkeley,
live with incongruity?)—but then the movie's sweet, spare music
chides me, and in the dark where no one can see I force my own
wry smile. I am offered a double irony: the people next door are
not really angry, the actors on the screen are not really in love—
so why be miffed? I tune out the martial scuffle; accommodation
is necessary for survival.

But back in the communal house a real fight is going on. Star
has accused Moonchild of stealing her cashew butter. (In Iowa,
my home, no one is named 'Star' or 'Moonchild.') The two are
circling in the living room, bent at the waist, crabstepping, backs
to walls, faces twisted into the horrible grimaces of Japanese

35

temple guardians. Star pays rent by peddling ugly jewelry on Telegraph Avenue. She has supple, ivory-pale fingers; she makes her jewelry with these same exquisite fingers, but I do not understand how they can fashion such squashed, hideous shapes. Why do people buy her wares? Star is tall, angular, with a thatch of close-cropped wheaten hair, at which she keeps plucking as she screams. I hold my breath. I have never seen her so frantic.

"The whole thing! You ate the whole fucking thing!" she shrills at Moonchild. "The second shelf of the fridge is *mine*, you know it is, but you just can't stay out of my space, you bastard!"

Suddenly there is a glint of metal; Star's long arm lifts, throws. A knife? I cringe. But it is only a spoon. Moonchild ducks. The spoon strikes the wall very near my head—thunk!—and stays there, Exhibit A, firmly glued by cashew butter.

Moonchild emits a choked, unconvincing laugh. He is a black-haired, gnomish young man in leather pants and leather vest. His eyes are wild, and I half expect him to stick out his tongue, but I do not stay to watch. Head ducked, I creep toward the friendly creak of this big old house's broad old stairs, my room under the eaves—sanctuary. But before I can reach the first step, Moonchild's footfalls clatter at my heels; his thick, crankcase smell of auto garage engulfs me. "Idiot!" he mutters, jostling past, and the word seems to take in all of us—me, Star, himself. Tears on his cheeks? His muffled retreat echoes after him, a door slams hollowly, and, hand on the bannister, I abruptly stop. "*I love her* ..." It is Moonchild's thin, scared wail in my memory, chilling. A confidence which I did not look for. Her. Star. The young woman who has become a crushed, clenched presence behind me, sobbing. My fingers leap from the bannister. All at once its dark, worn mahogany seems to lead to dangerous regions, and I am flooded with anguish. Has Moonchild forfeited love by his depredations? Love. Cashew butter. I am forty, growing fat. Pondering, I force my bulk up stairs which seem newly intent on tripping me. Is there such a thing as sanctuary? Careful, careful, a voice whispers. Communal life may have been a bad choice, and perhaps, after all, it does not do to live so near.

Upstairs. Safe.

I am an agronomist. A visiting professor, I have come west

from Iowa State University.

There is not much agronomy at Berkeley, but what there is I take part in.

Berkeley startles me, geographically, psychologically. It is a foreign country. Iowa is flat; I am used to her golden summer heat and safe, generous expanses. One can see long distances in Iowa; one can, simply, see. But here the view is deceptive. Though part of Berkeley is flat—it is even called the flatlands—it is a pitiful flatness, the hills only waiting to shrug it into the Bay.

Maddeningly, everyone acknowledges the likelihood of the 'Big One,' but does nothing about it.

The housing office placed me in my communal home. "Only temporary," they said, and true to their word, discovered just days later a suitable apartment, but I had by that time made up my mind not to move. Slipping into my room, Moonchild had already hunkered miserably on the edge of my bed, grinding his hands together while he blurted his love story. Star had taken pains to warn me just what was and was not my space in the big, shared Frigidaire in the kitchen with the sticky, yellowed floor. (She had, in addition, like a peace offering, laid samples of her lumpy wares before me.) I had unpacked my books and met the two communal cats, Cheddar and Jack.

Connections had been made.

Moonchild pounds on my door. I know it is he because the door flies open before I can say "come in."

"Yes?" My greeting sounds silly, like a butler's absurd formality.

Moonchild's raggle-taggle black hair is even more disarrayed than usual. Stumbling in, he is a shattered presence whose tragedy seems to crowd every other object in my room into an airless cubic yard of space. "Shit!" he wails.

"Sit down?"

He glares at me through the hair, as if the suggestion is an insensitive affront. He displays his palms. "Cashew butter." The palms jiggle violently, and his amber eyes actually spin. "Fuckin' *cashew* butter!" He begins to charge around the room—here, there. One side is sloping ceiling and he cracks his head but does not seem to notice, and I remember the French love story, its soft focus and wry, gentle music: sanity.

SANCTUARY

Mrs. Parmalee bustles in from next door to say we are making too much noise. She is past middle age, butterball round. She dyes her hair but not skillfully; meant to be red, it is an odd pink color and stands out from her face in a mad frizz.

Mrs. Parmalee pretends to be sweet, kind, but I know that she punishes her parakeet by placing him in a glass jar and rolling him around on her floor.

"Mind your own business!" Moonchild screeches at her.

Even I start at his outburst.

Mrs. Parmalee squawks, vanishes. Running down like a toy, Moonchild sinks to a lotus position on the floor next to the bookcase—a wilting lotus. His job has something to do with motorcycles; there is always grease under his nails, and his stubby, greasy hands now curl like dead mice on the worn carpet in front of him. "Star...Star...," he moans.

Helplessly, I stare at this lost child while the autumn darkness gropes about the room. In Iowa I live alone. One would never guess, in Iowa, the trials of communal life.

Mrs. Parmalee has left my door open, and all at once Bill is standing there. I am not even sure of Bill's last name, but Bill sums him up. Lanky, easy, whisper-voiced, he is our house's Calming Presence. He has enormous hands, and the broadest, slowest smile I have ever seen. His gray eyes drink in Moonchild, me; his smile, punctuated by a large brown mole on his left cheek, takes its time. "Well, I guess we just need a house meeting, don't we?" he drawls. "Downstairs in half an hour."

He might be calling us to wash up for supper.

A house meeting is a serious matter. There is one every week, on Tuesdays at 7:30, but tonight is Wednesday. Disturbances in the house—"bad vibes" Bill would call them—require emergency meetings; nothing is left to fester. I admire this policy, but I have been a member of the house only five weeks, so tonight will be my first chance to see how the policy functions. Will Star and Moonchild work out their cashew butter dispute?

It does not seem auspicious that, as we settle, murmuring in a circle on the old furniture in the beam-ceilinged living room, the spoon still hangs on the wall by the door, a little metal question mark glued by brown glop.

There is Bill, me, Moonchild, Star; also Dulcie Orhbach, the aloof, voluptuous young woman who lives in the room next to mine (on sleepless nights I imagine her breathing through the wall.) Dulcie crosses spectacular honey-brown legs. Bernie Kaplan rushes in. An enormous walrus moustache hides his upper lip, and his balding, furrowed brow looks damper than usual. Bernie is a law student at Boalt. Plopping onto a cushion, he emits a resentful sigh. "So what's this?" he demands of no one in particular, then catches sight of the spoon, and his round, nervous face screws up suspiciously.

Mrs. Parmalee plumps in last, radiating a mood of tight-fisted hostility, and I fear things will not go well for her parakeet tonight.

"Well, now." Cross-legged on a hassock, Bill is smiling, nodding at each person. His dewy look is more benign than ever, and I anticipate one of his "trip" exercises, where he insists we close our eyes while he tells us we are in a glade and should let butterflies' wings caress our cheeks while tension drains out our fingertips. But this is not trip time. "So. There are some bad vibes in our house," he says, scratching his nose, "and we just have to get rid of them."

I feel disloyal, thinking of *The Exorcist*: shaking beds, revolving heads, green vomit.

"Alice—?" Bill gently encourages.

Alice Permalee is a rock of resentment. "He—," a finger jabbed in Moonchild's direction, "told me to mind my own business!"

"Well, you ought to." Bernie Kaplan's moustache puffs in and out as he speaks.

Alice clutches her bosom—actually grasps a plump breast in each hand. "Augh!" she gasps.

"Good, good," Bill says, still smiling, eyes almost vanished under sand-colored lashes. "Get those feelings out."

"You...shit!" Alice spits at Bernie, giving up all pretense at sweetness, kindness.

Dulcie shifts her long legs. To Alice she says, "You shit too. We all shit. What's this about? I've got a date." In a bored, languid manner she tosses shoulder-length blue-black hair, while Alice grips her breasts even tighter, as if they are water wings that will keep her afloat in this sea of betrayal.

"Moonchild ate my cashew butter," Star puts in with a small, deeply serious pucker of frown. She plucks at her wheaten tufts. "That's what's important. Space is the issue. We all have to stay out of one another's space. Otherwise this house thing won't work. We have to respect the other person's space. Moonchild just doesn't respect mine, that's all." Wanly, she adds, "Maybe I should move out."

"Oh, no, honey," Dulcie says, reaching across to tap Star's knee. She glowers wickedly at Moonchild. "Let the *thief* do the moving."

Moonchild's lower lip trembles.

"Cashew butter?" Bernie explodes, and Bill looks delighted, his eyes now completely sunk behind the sandy lashes, his face a Buddha's mask. "We're here because of *cashew butter?*" Bernie's voice sounds strangled. "We oughta have a meeting about *your* nitpicking," he snarls at Star. "Space, Christ! Here—" he charges out, there is a rattle-bang from the kitchen, then he is back, thrusting a jar in Star's face, "—here, take mine, I don't care!"

Star wrinkles her nose. "It's *peanut* butter. Ugh! Jiff! Sugar, salt, hydrogenated vegetable oil . . ."

"Take the label, too," Bernie says. "*Eat* the goddamn label!" In a fury, Moonchild is suddenly on his feet. "Don't...don't you say that to her!" He punches Bernie's shoulder.

The jar plummets to the floor: crack!

The sound makes all of us jump.

Bernie stares at the jar, at Moonchild. In disbelief he sinks back on his cushion, rubbing his shoulder, and his mouth hangs open.

Alice holds onto her breasts.

Moonchild looks horrified.

Peanut butter begins to seep onto the rug.

Star is weeping. "Oh, it's all my fault, all my fault...!"

Now Bill is frowning. "This is a non-violent house," he chides Moonchild. "We—"

"What about *verbal* violence?" Moonchild yelps in Bill's face, black hair dancing. "That's okay?"

An alert, tawny tail darts around the sofa, and all at once Cheddar is among us, sniffing at the leaking peanut butter,

40

making small, sticky, lapping sounds.

"Oh, go 'way!" Alice relinquishes her breasts long enough to flip her hands at the cat.

Star glares at her. "You've *always* hated Cheddar!"

Alice's hands fly back to her breasts. Her round eyes gush tears. "You want him to eat *glass*?"

"It's the hydrogenated vegetable oil she's worried about," Bernie puts in snidely, still rubbing his shoulder. "Star, sweetheart, your boyfriend is a son of a bitch."

"He's not my boyfriend!" It is a frustrated wail.

"Am too!" Moonchild desperately insists.

A membrane of silence stretches over us, but it is taut, ready to explode. Cheddar's tawny coat bristles. Bernie's moustache puffs in and out. Star tugs at her hair, while Dulcie groans and rolls her eyes.

"We haven't heard from Peter yet," Bill says at last, in a sly, silken voice, and all eyes fall on me.

I admire Bill's ploy; I hate it. I swallow. My mouth attempts a grin, but my lips desert my will. My housemates wait—even Cheddar watches—and it is as if I am the guilty party, the catalyst for this grating, abrasive event; last to join the house, I have tipped their volatile mixture toward disaster. "Uh—." My throat will not work. I cannot say what I think. I know my mind, just cannot utter it.

"I'm going to the movies," I tell them abruptly, rise, and bang out the big oak door into Berkeley.

Cool, bay-scented air fans my face. The October night is feathery with dark. Listening to my rapid, escaping footfalls plopping downhill as if they are someone else's, I am amazed, then pleased at my nerve. I laugh out loud: such wonderful, blatant rudeness! (Of course, in Iowa it would not be necessary.) I imagine six outraged expressions. At least I have united them. I have walked out on a communal meeting. Will they ask me to leave for good?

I make a mental note to visit the housing office tomorrow.

My feet are leading me toward the dangerous flatlands of Berkeley, but I feel reckless; I know where I am going. It takes me half an hour to reach the odd little theater again. The third and last showing is about to begin, and, ticket in hand (an airline ticket, I pretend), I, a passenger, enter the theater and am whisked to France. Next door the judo school is still in full swing—thud! whack!—but the sounds thoroughly please me, and I settle back, happy for the time being to be where love and violence are not real.

DEAD BOY'S FAREWELL
Kirsten and Ray Nelson

SINCE I DIED I feel so much better. If an anxiety lingers, it is to fix the time of death, the year, the month, the week, the hour, the exact second. Such quiet now surrounds me, such peace, and in that peace, so like a white shifting, drifting fog, events glow and flicker like red embers in a dying fire, like brief sparks that blaze and drop and are gone. Soon I will see only smoke, and will know nothing at all.

Was it at the Villa Diodati on the shore of Lake Geneva in Switzerland that sunny afternoon in 1923? Mama had driven like a madwoman as usual, but we were used to it, Aunt Denise, Anna my governess, and I. Mama always talked as she drove, turning her head to direct a remark to me or to Anna in the back seat, or to Aunt Denise beside her. She spoke at length and with approval of Benito Mussolini, who had recently taken power in Italy at the invitation of the King. Mussolini, she said repeatedly, had at least made the trains run on time, a fact we could attest to, as our rail journey from Rome to Geneva, were we had picked up the car Father had bought for us, had been singularly pleasant and uneventful. I still hear the high scream of the whistle echoing, as if from a great distance, still hear the clattering wheels, the murmur of the Italian family who shared our compartment. I can still smell the stench of their garlic breath, still see in my imagination the way they touched each other. How can such filthy people bring themselves to touch each other once, let alone repeatedly? I had to look away or be ill.

But now Mama spoke with emphasis. "If the trains run on time, a nation is well on the way to order."

Aunt Denise nodded.

Anna said nothing.

When Mama was delivering one of her monologues, we knew

43

better than to interrupt, even to agree. I stared at the mountains, so white and cold. I like things that are white and cold. I paid no attention to Mama until she called my name.

"Gordon!"

"Yes, Mama."

"You will be interested in the place we are about to visit."

"Yes, Mama."

"The man you were named after once lived there. George Gordon, whom you may know, if you paid attention to your tutor, as Lord Byron. I wouldn't have chosen to name you after such a person, a man who, for all his fame, led a far from respectable life. Your father fancied the name. Your father thought himself a poet, you know. Can you imagine such a thing? We will be visiting the very house in which Lord Byron disported himself with a tart named Claire Claremont, who later bore him a daughter out of wedlock."

Aunt Denise took advantage of a break in the flow as Mama returned the car to the proper side of the road. "Should we tell such a thing to a young boy?"

"A priest must know the ways of the world," Mama answered primly.

She braked to a stop and turned off the motor. The dust we had raised swirled around us for a moment as Mama gathered herself together. "Follow me," she commanded, and opened the door.

I see us in my imagination, a small black parade, four insects in a line marching through the cold still air. We all wore black. We always wore black. We were all thin, bony, pale, unsmiling.

"I will have something to tell you," said Mama to me. "Prepare yourself."

"Tell me now," I said.

"No. Later."

We approached an ancient three-storied house with a gabled roof that glistened wetly in the sunlight. In spite of the bright sun, we could see our breath, feel the dampness of a recent storm. Mama consulted her guidebook, then said, "On May 23, 1816, at 9 p.m., during a frightful downpour, five young friends huddled together in this house, reading ghost stories out loud. Lord Byron, then already steeped in scandal, his mistress Claire Claremont, his friend Dr. John Polidori, the poet Percy Shelly, and

Shelly's mistress, Mary Godwin, whom he later married after his wife's suicide. They decided to try their hand at making up tales of horror of their own. Polidori's *The Vampire* became the model for the Bram Stoker tale, *Dracula*. Byron and Shelly began tales they never completed, and Mary Godwin, inspired by a frightful nightmare, began *Frankenstein*. You've always liked that book, Gordon."

"Yes, Mama."

Aunt Denise said, "You should never have let him read such stuff."

"His father insisted he be given the run of the family library. What could I do?"

Aunt Denise fixed me with a dark, glittering eye. "Gordon, what do you see in such rubbish?"

"I find it amusing, Auntie."

"Amusing! I declare!" Aunt Denise sniffed contemptuously. "A murdering monster? Amusing?"

"He wasn't at fault," I told her. "He was made of flesh, you know. Everything fleshly is sinful."

Mama said approvingly, "You see, Denise? He's already a priest in his heart! I've always known he would be a priest."

"A priest?" Aunt Denise looked at me, her face a white, expressionless mask. "He could be a cardinal, a Pope."

Encouraged, I added, "The name of God is not once mentioned in *Frankenstein*. The author never takes the name of the Lord in vain."

"I imagine that's because this heathen woman doesn't believe in God," said Aunt Denise.

"She believes in God," I said quietly. "The real God."

"Is there a real God and a false God?" Aunt Denise demanded.

"Oh yes," I replied.

Mama leaned forward to catch my words, as if I were already a Pope, speaking *ex cathedra*.

"The false God is the God of the Flesh," I told her. "The real God is the God of the Spirit. The real God lives far, far away. He is very cold and white, like a mountain. Around Him everything is quiet. Around Him there is snow, and white clouds, and nothing moves. He does not understand pain. He does not know about suffering. He is never lonely. He watches us. He watches

45

us and does nothing." An odd sensation came over me, a sensation I have felt more and more often recently. "Like you, Mama.
Like you, Auntie. You watch me and do nothing."

"What a thing to say!" cried Aunt Denise. "You should be
punished! After all we do for you!" I wasn't afraid. They would
never spank me. To spank me they would have to touch me.

"You cannot punish me," I said quietly.

For once Mama was at a loss for words. Anna looked at me
with concern. Anna was concerned for me. She was paid to be
concerned for me.

"The monster wasn't at fault," I said. "His maker was at
fault."

None of the three women contradicted me. Behind their white,
mask-like faces I thought I detected a flicker of fear, as if I were
the monster myself. I liked making them afraid.

We continued the tour. I felt quietly powerful.

As we returned to the limousine, Mama said, "Have you prepared yourself, Gordon?"

"For what, Mama?"

"For what I have to tell you."

"Yes, Mama."

"Your father and I have separated, Gordon."

I stared at her, feeling nothing.

She went on. "You and I will stay in Italy. We will live in
Rome, you and I. Aunt Denise and Anna will live with us."

The three women watched my face for some reaction. I watched
the mountains and the clouds. The clouds were tall and white. I
said nothing.

Aunt Denise said, "Your mother and I have always believed in
you, Gordon. We have always believed you were destined for
higher things. If you had stayed in America, the power of Mam-
mon would have corrupted your soul. The materialism of your
father would have made you a money-grubbing philistine like
the rest of the men in our family. We couldn't let that happen to
you."

I spoke without emotion. "Will I ever see my father again?"

Mama answered, "We think it best you not see him. The
distraction—it might upset you. You will be so busy with your
studies. You will go to a special school in Rome. You will study

to be a priest. You always were interested in religion."

"Yes," I said. "I have a calling."

Relief showed in their faces. I was brave. I took it well.

Was that when I died?

We drove to Geneva and registered at a huge white hotel.

Anna and I walked in the hotel gardens the next day. It was sunny and cold, as before, but I did not feel the cold. I seldom notice if it is hot or cold.

Anna said, "If you feel like crying, I won't tell."

"I don't feel like crying."

"Won't you miss your father?"

"I hardly ever saw him. He was always so busy. And why would anything happen to me if I cried? What difference would it make if you told?"

"Perhaps you don't remember." Anna looked at me intently. "Oh, Gordon, I never know what you feel, what you think, what you remember."

"I don't feel anything."

"Do you remember when you were little? The big yard with all the expensive toys?"

"Yes, of course."

"You had no playmates. I thought you might be lonely. I gave you a kitten to keep you company. Do you remember?"

"No, Anna."

"You were happy for a while. You laughed. You actually laughed. But you were...awkward. The kitten died. Don't you remember?"

"No." I felt a growing uneasiness.

"You wept. You wept for two days. Don't you remember? Your mother commanded you to stop, but you didn't. She preached to you to accept the will of God. She preached to you that kittens had no souls. She preached to you that you would never be a priest if you lacked courage. Don't you remember?"

"No. Don't tell my any more."

"Does it make you sad?"

"No."

"You had many servants then, not just me. They were forbidden to touch you. Your mother thought they might do something dirty to you. As you sat in the yard in your sandbox screaming, one of them, a Scandinavian named Kirsten, tiptoed out to you and picked you up and hugged you. Then she gave you a glass of water. You stopped screaming. Don't you remember?"

"No." I felt water coming out, as if out of someone else's eyes, running down someone else's cheek.

She knelt down beside me, staring into my face. "I see tears on your cheek, but you're not crying," she said, amazed.

"It's a very sad story," I said coldly as the tears continued. "You might as well finish telling it."

"Your mother came running out into the yard, livid with rage, and fired Kirsten on the spot. Then she stood over you and looked down at you and did nothing, and you stared up at her. I don't think I've heard you weep again since."

I wondered: Did I die then?

After a long silence I said, "I can tell stories too, Anna. Have you ever heard of reincarnation?"

"That's a heathen idea!"

"Some people remember past lives. I do. But it's not what people think. It's someone else in my body. Someone else remembers other lives. Someone else remembers ancient Rome, the building of the pyramids, the hunting of the saber-toothed tiger. When someone is lonely enough, sometimes someone comes to keep him company. "

"I don't understand." She seemed totally bewildered.

I said gravely, "If I do something to you, forgive me. It is only to save your life. And don't worry about me, Anna. I'm not a human being."

With that I broke away from her and ran, screaming, through the gardens, the lush, beautiful gardens, and ladies and gentlemen turned to watch me, amazed. "Mama!" I screamed. "Auntie Denise!"

Then I saw Mama and Aunt Denise descending the broad marble staircase from the hotel entrance, and they too stared at me as I ran toward them shouting.

"What is it, Gordon?" Mama asked sharply.

"Calm yourself. Tell us what's wrong," said Aunt Denise as she shrank back, afraid I would touch her.

I panted, "Anna tried to put her hand inside my pants!"

48

The next day we started for the mountains.

Mama explained that we would work our way along the coast of Lake Geneva, then thread our way through the Alps to Italy, where we would proceed to Rome and settle down. They had already enrolled me in a special school there.

As we drove away from the hotel I said, "Where's Anna?"

"On her way back to the states," answered Mama grimly.

"Will we see her again?" I asked.

"You poor innocent baby. Of course not."

We stopped at an inn along the shore for lunch.

The dining room was decorated with potted flowers, potted flowers everywhere.

"How beautiful!" Aunt Denise exclaimed.

"It's like a funeral," Mama answered with distaste.

I said nothing.

"I'm glad you told us about Anna," she said to me. "You mustn't keep things like that to yourself. You might turn out to be like your namesake, Lord Byron. They say he was molested as a child, and that's why he chose a life of sin."

"He did no wrong," I said calmly.

"How can you say that?" Mama asked coldly. "Do you know all the things he's said to have done?"

"He did nothing," I insisted. "It wasn't him."

"Who then?"

"A spirit within him."

"How do you know that?"

"I am that spirit."

Mama looked at me uneasily, a little afraid. I liked the fear in her eyes.

Aunt Denise put in quickly, "The boy is upset. Don't pay any attention to what he says."

After lunch we went for a walk along the shore.

Lake Geneva was a perfect mirror, reflecting the cold, distant mountains. The docks, where little white boats rode at anchor, were deserted. We crossed a wooden footbridge that led to a placid inlet covered with water lilies.

Mama said, "Hired girls are always chancy. This is the second one that's let me down."

Aunt Denise said, "But we can't get along without them." She

49

sighed in patient martyrdom.

"Perhaps we can, Denise," said Mama.

"And you and I do all the work? Oh no."

"He's not a baby, and he'll be at school most of the time."

"I came along on the understanding that we'd have servants. What do you think I am?"

"If you won't help, I'll do it all myself."

"That'll be the day!"

"I can do it. I don't need you."

"You always have needed me. You've always depended on me."

"Depended on you? For what?"

"To cover up, for one thing."

"To cover up what, Denise?"

"For the boy. You know very well what I mean. He's not normal. We both know that."

"Not normal? He's just more spiritual than other children, that's all. He has a calling, that's all."

"A calling? From who? God, or someone else?"

"How dare you say such things, Denise? Traitor!"

Aunt Denise had come to the end of the narrow wooden pier. She turned to face us. Behind her floated the dark green lily pads and a few pink and white blossoms. I thought about how strong lilies are, how things are woven from their stems, how people sometimes become entangled in them. I thought how none of us could swim.

Suddenly, without warning, I dashed forward and threw my full weight against Aunt Denise.

She was so thin, so light. She fell easily, screaming only a little. If I had not caught my balance I would have tumbled in after her.

As I had expected, she became entangled. She did not struggle long. Mama and I watched her, doing nothing.

At last Mama whispered, "Oh God, what have you done?"

I told her gently, "We don't need her. Now it's just you and I."

She clasped and unclasped her hands. "Yes. Yes. Just you and I." Then she smiled. Just for an instant. I could not recall ever having seen her smile before.

Then we went for help.

The funeral delayed us only a week. It had been an accident. The poor woman had fallen in, and neither I nor Mama had been able to swim. An accident.

We buried Auntie in an unmarked grave.

Then we continued on our tour.

As we wended our way up the hairpin turns into the Alps, higher, ever higher, I felt nearer and nearer to that distant deity who sits in splendor in the cold stillness, whose throne is on a glacier between two white mountain peaks where no wind blows and nothing breathes, that great God who never hungers, never thirsts, never feels the need of any other being but is content to be eternally alone, alone, alone. I prayed to Him, who hears no prayers. I worshipped Him, who needs no worship. I adored Him, who loves no one.

But no trace of my ecstasy did I permit to show on my face, nor did I let my lips betray my wordless longing by so much as an unguarded murmur, a careless sigh.

With screaming tires, the car rounded one bend after another. Mama talked endlessly of the future, of my future. My secret was safe with her. I would study hard. I would rise in the Church. I would wear red robes, a red hat. I would choose the Pope. I would be the Pope.

An accident! It had been an accident! We couldn't let a moment's carelessness destroy a wonderful career.

We reached the crest of the first range of mountains and started down.

"Be careful, Mama," I whispered, to be fair. "Not so fast."

"I know how to drive," she snapped, looking toward me as I sat beside her. The tires crunched on the soft shoulder before she swung us back on the road.

"Let me help you, Mama." I grasped the steering wheel.

"No, Gordon! No!" The terror made her white mask of a face almost human.

We went over the cliff. We seemed to fly. The land and the sky traded places.

Was that when I died?

I open my eyes. A man with a white mask over his mouth looks down at me, a bright light above him framing his face like a halo.

51

I say, "Where am I?"

He answers, "San Francisco General Hospital. You tried to kill yourself, buddy."

"A car?"

"No, sleeping pills."

"What time is it?"

"Ten at night."

"No, I mean what year?"

"May, 1983."

When did I die? Never! And I never will.

The cold white mountains remain on the horizon, and the being who lives there remains in meditation on His throne, no closer and no further away than He has ever been or ever will be.

EGGS
Marko

"Love is like frying an egg: Breaking the shell is just the beginning."

Mother likes to tell me things like that. As much as I love my parents, I have to admit that they were always more than a little prone to clichés. Mother has probably gotten worse since Dad died four years ago. My stepfather is a fine fellow, but he subscribes to the *Reader's Digest*. I don't think that has helped.

From time to time, my friends accuse me of being obsessive. That is, I get interested in something and refuse to let go of it until I'm through. Mom's the same way. My father used to do all the cooking around the house. After he died, mother got it into her head that it would be easier for me if she learned to cook. That way, even though Dad was gone, I'd still eat just as well when I came home.

Right now, she's making breakfast. She woke me up at seven this morning so I could have Danish, fresh orange juice, a short stack of pancakes, blueberry muffins, four link sausages, and three eggs. She also tried to convince me to have a bowl of soup left over from last night, but Don, my stepfather, and I managed to unite and talk her out of that one. Nonetheless, there is still a pot of soup on the table. Mother believes in soup every day. It's good for you.

I haven't combed my hair yet. Mother gets upset about such things.

"I wake up just to cook you breakfast. The least you can do is groom yourself in the morning. You don't have to look at yourself."

Sometimes it's hard to humor your mother at seven in the morning. Especially when you've stayed up until four.

"This is my house. You live by my rules. In your own place,

you do whatever you want," she tells me. I grunt.

I've often wondered how eggs got to be a breakfast food. When you burn them, they won't come off the pan. Egg yolk stays on plates forever. It's gooey and slippery. You can never tell when eggs are done properly. The shells stink if you leave them in the garbage too long. Still, as I smell the eggs frying on the stove, I know that they must, for some reason, be included in every home-cooked breakfast, just like my mother's soup.

I haven't decided whether I should tell her about Kristen. Actually, she already knows about Kristen. I brought her home once about a year ago.

"This is the woman I intend to marry. I want your approval," I told her.

I told her in that way sons tell their mothers such things. That is, I beamed a lot, offered to do the dishes, combed my hair before breakfast, and kept asking her, "Well, what do you think?"

"What do I think of what?" she teased me back. "She seemed nice. I only met her just for a while."

It meant that Mom sort of liked her, but not really a whole lot.

"You really love her, don't you?" she asked me a few days later.

"I've never felt this way about anyone else," I told her.

Mother nodded her head and mumbled something about all the fish in the sea. Two weeks later, Kristen dropped me because she wanted to marry someone else. Mother knew, because of a single sentence in Kristen's thank-you note: "You know, I care about Malcolm very much."

Mother conveniently lost the letter.

"She was probably afraid because of your being Chinese. She couldn't tell you something like that."

Every time I break up with a white girlfriend, Mother is convinced that that's the reason. I never told her that Kristen's previous boyfriend was black. Mom always warns me about bringing home any black girlfriends.

The eggs match the kitchen table. Everything in our kitchen is white with a touch of yellow. Mom likes bright colors, new things. The Cuisinart is white, the stovetop is white, the new refrigerator with the ice cube dispenser on the outside is white. The chopsticks, the rice, and Mom and Don and myself are yellow. The placemats are white with printed yellow daisies. It seems that Mom changes placemats every time I come home.

"Waste of money," I tell her, parroting my father.

About a third of the time this gets her very upset.

"It's not your money. You just don't have any feel for the way things look. They cheer me up," she'll snap.

This morning, she doesn't react.

I've decided that mothers and sons get a certain pleasure out of irritating each other. When you know just the right way to do it, it's almost impossible to resist. This kind of irritation reminds you that you share some extreme intimacy. It sounds incredibly perverse, but over the years I've begun to realize that small doses of it are actually sort of healthy.

It's one of those things which made Kristen someone special. Right away, we knew exactly how to bug each other. I suppose that is a little worse than perverse. It even sounds vaguely oedipal. The only way to explain it is that we immediately communicated in some manner which ordinarily would have taken years to develop. I guess my parents aren't the only ones who are prone to clichés. Whatever the cliché, it's made it impossible for us to give up on each other. Months later, we're still talking about getting back together.

"Get rid of the bitch," Byron told me. Byron, my best friend, decided five years ago, at the age of twenty one, that all women were basically neurotic. He's really not a misogynist as much as he's a skeptic. For some frustrating reason, he is right a lot of the time. Of course, I've never told him that. On the other hand, he hasn't had a girlfriend in six years.

"Malcolm, you deserve better than that," Lori insisted. Lori has always been not so secretly in love with me.

"What are you going to do? She can't make up her mind. She could walk off one morning on you." Mother finally advised me, "There are a lot of birds in the forest."

"Don't you mean fish in the sea?"

"Birds, fish. Why don't you drink your soup? You don't eat very much anymore."

"You don't really understand," I tried to tell each one of them, "I can't really explain it."

In each case, of course, I spent several hours trying to explain it anyway. Byron shook his head a lot and said something about how he had finally concluded that worrying about one's friends was patronizing. Lori told me that she really worried about me. Mother started teasing me about another one of my old girlfriends.

"Whatever happened to so and so, the one who lived in Sonora or Twain Harte, wherever that was? She was going to let us stay in her cabin."

I drink some more orange juice. I try to sneak a glance at the morning sports page, but Mother gives me a dirty look.

"You can look at the newspaper later. I don't cook breakfast so you can spend the time with your head buried in the paper. Talk, eat, talk!"

She always expects me to somehow manage to do both at the same time.

Don smiles. I shake my head. We both know that there is nothing to do about it.

"Menopause. It's making you old and crotchety," I grumble.

"Why are you always trying to make me older than I am?" Mom answers, her voice taking on a girlish tinge.

"You told me to talk. What do you want me to talk about? I come home and Don's looking at all these catalogs for rest homes. I'm not the only one," I tell her.

Don and my mother both start laughing. They've got a good marriage. They talk, they tease each other, they do things together, and they have that aura which lets me know that they've come to rely on each other emotionally. All happy couples seem to have it. It's like the buckeyes and little wolves on the sides of the player's helmets at Midwestern football factories. You can always spot the stars.

"You know that is for Don's father, not me."

"Have you found one for him? Does he like it?" I ask him, genuinely interested.

We start talking. I start on the pancakes.

"How can you eat pancakes without butter?"

I shrug.

"God, you're too lazy to go get the butter yourself."

I turn to Don. "How much a month did you say that rest home cost?"

Don picks up the catalog and starts half-seriously going over the prices with me. Mother brings over the butter and I immediately dump a glob of it on my pancakes. She wants to talk. Mother always wants to talk.

I want to talk too, but at the moment all I want to talk about is Kristen.

"I hear Linda's got a new boyfriend."

Don nods. Linda is my stepsister. We're the same age, but have little in common except parents who are married to each other.

"What's he like?"

"Nice fellow. He's an engineer at Hewlett Packard or something," Mother answers. "Good-looking guy."

"He's even Japanese," Don adds smiling.

I look up, a bit surprised. "Does Linda like him?"

"I guess so," he shrugs.

"Are you seeing anyone these days?" Mother asks.

I look down and shake my head.

"We were going to fix you up with Don's niece. She's not too good-looking, but she's very nice." Mother pauses as I make a face. "You don't have to marry her. You can just go out, you know."

"I talked to Kristen."

This time Mother's head drops. "You're still talking." Pause. "How is she?"

"Okay, I guess."

"You mean she isn't getting married?"

"It didn't work out, I guess."

"You're not getting back together again, are you?"

Mom has a way of spotting my reactions before I can cover them up.

"God, she really put you through the wringer."

I shake my head as I try to escape from what I've started by biting into a blueberry muffin. The dog, a Welsh terrier which Mother feeds and pampers when Don and I are not around, is barking at me, demanding his share of my breakfast.

"Oh, give him something. You're not home that often."

Mother always talks to the dog in baby talk. She wanted more kids after me, but had cancer of the uterus not long after I was born. The family has been haunted by sudden illnesses. Mother's father died from leukemia when she was thirteen. Father, who she always refers to as "Dad", had a stroke. Our two previous dogs died from bizarre diseases. Even Don was exposed to one of those pesticides with the alphabetical names which always seem to be an acronym for cancer. In any case, Mom slips the dog a huge piece of sausage, something which unfailingly causes it to bark for more food.

We talk about the dogs, a favorite safe subject. Don won my mother over when he took the dog along on their first date. Apparently, Don, has finally managed to curb Alfred from bringing dead birds into the house.

"Do you remember that huge rat?"

"Oh God, that was terrible," Mother makes a face.

More silence.

"You know, son, there are plenty of flowers in the garden."

"I thought Alfred ate them all."

"You know what I mean."

"I guess some flowers are different from the others."

"There are going to be a lot more Kristens before you get through."

Don nods his head. He always stays out of these mother-son exchanges.

"Are you going to go gossip with all your old bat friends again today?"

"Yes, I'm going to sewing class again. They are pretty old, aren't they?" She looks up as if gazing into a mirror.

"Most of them must be pushing seventy. You're still just sixty-two."

"Fifty-two," she corrects me reflexively.

Mother goes to four sewing classes a week. Three months ago, she bought a fifteen hundred dollar sewing machine. Before that, it was golf. There are four old sets of clubs in the garage, leaning against the two extra freezers.

"You know, twenty years ago, all our friends were Chinese. Now, they're all white." She says it pensively, not really sure whether that's a good thing or a bad thing.

"Mom, do you really think Kristen got cold feet because I am Chinese?"

She looks up, away from me, out towards the morning sun. Every once in a while, I am forced to admit that my mother is a very good-looking woman. As the sun sifts through the kitchen shutters, I look at her even features, her freckled skin which somehow still has not wrinkled. More than anything else, it is the way she carries herself. She was totally dependent on my father; then she lost him, and managed to rebuild her life. Her life has not been filled with big challenges, but she has always been a match for the ones she had to face. She smiles.

"It probably didn't make it any easier."

"Did it bother you that she was white?"

She shakes her head. "I'd prefer that you came home with an Oriental," she starts out. "I think things would be a lot easier, but as long as she loves you . . .and can give me lots of grandchildren." She makes a face. "Just so long as you don't bring home any black ones."

I turn to Don, who has been quietly eating his pancakes. "Have you told her about your black grandfather?"

Don laughs. Mother doesn't.

"Mom?"

"Yes, son?"

"Isn't there any way to know?"

She shakes her head again, looks first at Don, then at me, and sighs.

I stick a fork into my eggs. The yolks run all over the shiny white plate.

THE BRIDES OF PROSPECT AVENUE
Lili Artel

My friend, Thelma Pearl, was the daughter of a Rabbi, I of a butcher turned traveling salesman for a supplier of *trayf* meat. One Saturday afternoon, I asked my mother: "How come if dad was a *trayf* butcher you married him?"

I was being spiteful. All my friends, except Thelma Pearl, spent Saturday afternoons at the Congress movie theater. Because it was the Sabbath, I could not carry money. No double feature plus serials for me.

"You're so religious and he's like a *goy*. How'j you two ever get together?"

Mama didn't look up from raking the *challah* crumbs from the white cloth covering the kitchen table. "Through a *shadchan*."

"But how could you marry him when he sold meat Jews can't eat?"

"So . . .?" Had it been any day other than Saturday, she would surely have slapped me, but slapping would have disrupted the Sabbath peace.

Mama sat down at the kitchen table and looked out at the Sabbath-hushed street one floor below. With the kids at the movies, there were no games of potsy or stickball. The neighbor women were off either shopping on Prospect Avenue or visiting family in other Bronx tenements. The men had the day off, except for my father and Mr. Cassidy on the top floor.

"Aren't you goin' over to Thelma's?" Mama asked after a while.

"What for? We can't do nothin'."

"So go for a walk on Prospect Avenue."

"Big deal."

Thelma opened the door. "Hi," she said glumly. We went to

her room, sat down on the bed covered with a pink chenille spread. I knew I'd have to pick pink balls of fuzz off my blue crepe dress.

"A new dress?" Thelma asked.

"Not really. Got it for New Year's but wore it only for 'good.' Now Mama says I'd better get some wear out of it." I looked down; the bodice strained across my chest. I'd filled out since September. "But your dress is new."

Thelma glanced down as if she'd forgotten what she wore.

"Tear it in good health. Stand up, Thel, and spin around so the skirt flares out."

"I don't feel like spinning."

"What'samatta you're so blah?"

"I've got the 'curse.' I had such cramps yesterday I couldn't go to school. You're lucky you don't have it."

"So . . . sooner or later . . . ." I rose from the bed and began picking the pink lint off my dress. "How come when it's May, your mom makes you a high-necked, long-sleeved dress?"

"It's a style I like."

"Who'ya kiddin'?"

Thelma tossed her head. "It's Asher's idea."

"Who's Asher?"

"Who's Asher?" She mimicked me. "When ya gonna remember that Asher's the assistant Rabbi who came from Poland to help my father when he got sick."

"Oh. Him! The one who sneaks a look at you sideways and won't shake hands with a woman."

"Asher's shy; besides he's a *Chassid*."

"Boy, is he filling up your head with pious stuff."

"What pious stuff?"

"Like not taking off all your clothes when you bathe."

"Oh that. Well, when a girl's body changes and she gets the 'curse,' she should be more modest. So what if you take a bath in a slip."

"Fine. You wash the slip at the same time."

"Leah, have you got somethin' against Asher?"

"Yeah. I do. If not for him, you'd still be going to *Cheder* and I wouldn't have to be the only girl in class. Why did he talk your mom into taking you out? 'Cause a girl don't need a Hebrew education since she can't be *bar mitzvahed?*"

"Finished, Miss Smarty? He wanted to help my mother save money by tutoring me himself."

I wasn't going to back down. "Whether I like Asher or not don't matter. I think Asher don't like girls."

"You've got a lot of nerve. Asher's like one of the family now that my brother Moish is studying in Poland . . .and my Papa's dead," she added in a whisper.

"I'm sorry, but I didn't mean Asher's a fairy."

"Forget it," Thelma said petulantly.

"Okay. Shall we go for our walk?"

A stroll along Prospect Avenue to check out the bridal salons was a Sabbath ritual. Thelma went to the kitchen to tell her mom we were leaving. I waited in the foyer. A band of sunlight fell across one wall spotlighting the wedding picture that hung there. I moved closer to study it. It was a threesome: bride, groom and the groom's mother—Thelma's parents and grandmother, who was the central figure in the photograph. She sat in a straight-backed armchair, staring sternly into the camera. A black lace scarf matching the black lace dress was draped over her matron's wig. In her earlobes were tiny diamonds. The only other piece of jewelry she wore was a gold wedding band.

The bride, posed sideways (to the left of the old woman), held her head turned full-face toward the camera. A tiara, covered in seed pearls, sat atop a crown of her own black braids. Sprigs of seed pearls spangled the long-sleeved, white taffeta gown and the floor-length veil.

To the right of his mother, the groom looked straight out of the picture through steel-rimmed glasses. A mustache and trimmed beard barely concealed his surprisingly full lips. He appeared to be short legged, but it could have been the effect of the cutaway coat he wore.

I'd become so engrossed in the picture that I was startled to find Thelma asking me if I wanted something to drink. I went to the kitchen. "*Gut Shabbas*, Mrs. Silberstein."

"*Gut Shabbas*, Leah. You want some milk?"

"No, thank you. I can't have any; it isn't six hours yet after eating meat."

"Would you like some seltzer then?"

"Yes." I watched her spritz some into a glass, add a dollop of strawberry jam and fill the glass to the top with more seltzer. As I watched her, I thought: she's all in black...wears a matron's wig...the beautiful bride vanished...in her place a younger replica of her mother-in-law.

Mrs. Silberstein handed me the drink. "Thanks." I drank until the tickle up my nose made me pause. "You were a beautiful bride."

Mrs. Silberstein shrugged her right shoulder and tilted her head toward it. "All brides are beautiful."

I finished the drink and handed the glass back to her, saying I was afraid to put it down in the wrong place.

"The way your mama brings you up, you should marry a Rabbi. What surprises me is that your mama didn't marry one or at least a man who sells *kosher* meat."

"She fell in love with my father."

"Fell in love!" Mrs. Silberstein pressed her lips together and pushed them out. "In our generation, your mama's and mine, getting married came first, not falling in love. Love came after the wedding. And if it didn't...." She wagged her head from side to side slowly.

"*Gut voch*," I said to Mrs. Silberstein as Thelma and I shut the door behind us.

"Be careful crossing," she called after us from the window.

The bridal salons were on the sunny side of the Avenue. As we neared the first one, the proprietor was lowering the awning. We began our game: to pick a bridal gown for a June wedding. The bride dummy, dressed in a floor-length white silk gown with yards and yards of train in a circular sweep about her feet, looked like Venus rising from a frothy sea. A fingertip veil fell from a Juliet cap set upon her blonde wig. Cradled in her hands was a small bible in a gold case.

"I'd bust that tight bodice." I grinned.

"I don't have enough to fill it."

"Wear falsies."

Thelma glared at me.

At the next salon, the chiffon bridal gown was lavishly ruffled from neck to ankle. "I think it's too fussy," I said.

"I like it, but I couldn't wear short sleeves in a *shul* ceremony."

"Just add long white gloves."

"Right. I'll take it." Thelma giggled.

We strolled on to the next bridal shop, past the florist. In one window were bridal bouquets, arranged on display pedestals covered with silver paper. Above them dangled a cut-out cardboard Cupid, bow and arrow at the ready.

In the other display window were funeral wreaths.

Next we came to the showplace of the Avenue, Mme. Regina's. It had been converted from a home into a place of business when Madame became a widow. The facade was painted white and the four high, narrow windows of the front parlor had been replaced by one large plate glass window. An arched effect above the window made it look like a stage. Mauve velvet drapes framed the window like a stage curtain. A complete wedding party was on display.

Thelma and I hardly glanced at the groom in his white jacket with a red carnation in the lapel. We had eyes only for the bride, her gown in the Spanish mode. The skirt, comprised of tier upon tier of lace flounces, ended in a train like a peacock's tail. Upon her black, center-parted hair was a lace mantilla, held high by an ornate comb. The bouquet in her outstretched hand was a fall of orchids.

"You'd look great in this one, Thel." Thelma was tall and lanky and had straight black hair.

Thelma wrinkled her nose. "It's too, ummm . . . ."

As she fumbled for the right word, I said: "Sexy?"

"Yeah. I guess so."

"You like the little-girl-full-of-ruffles look, huh?"

"You don't have to get sarcastic. I gotta right to like what I like." She retreated into a huffy silence and we walked on to the next shop.

Here a white sheet had been stretched across the window; this was done when a display was being changed. One end of the sheet had fallen away to reveal an almost nude mannequin. Her slip was hitched up around her neck. She was bald. One arm and both hands had been removed; the latter rested in a corner of the window in a prayerful gesture. Though dismembered, the dummy kept smiling.

"Bet they're goin' outta business or they'da fixed the window up for Saturday."

"That's not why," Thelma said. "There's been a death in the owner's family."

"How do you know?"

Thelma pointed to the black crepe affixed to the store's door.

"Oh," I said. "Lissen. I haven't found a gown yet. Ya wanna go on?"

"D'you?"

"It's up to you."

Thelma turned homeward and I followed. After a while, I said: "Sometimes I feel phooey on all that fuss and feathers . . . ."

"So wear a white suit, a frilly blouse and a little pill box with a veil."

"That's not what I—"

Thelma cut in and the next thing I knew she was into the plot of a movie starring Ginger Rogers and Fred Astaire. Now Ginger worked in the bridal salon of a high class department store. In the next department, Fred played the piano promoting popular songs. "Never, never change . . . keep that breathless charm . . . ."

"Astaire's a lousy singer." I was annoyed with Thelma but I took it out on Astaire. Thelma wasn't fazed. She went right on to describe a dance number in which Ginger changed gowns in midstep. "It's like a dream and she's floating in a starry sky and the stars are Astaire's dancing feet."

"I'll admit Astaire's lighter than air on his feet."

Thelma ignored my remark and went on with the story. I was so peeved, I hardly listened. An elopement . . . a ceremony at the Justice of Peace . . . Ginger wearing the suit she wears to work . . . Fred buying her a bunch of white violets . . . .

I tuned in again just in time to contradict her. "Violets are purple."

"There are white ones too. They're mutants."

Thelma was always pulling stuff like that because she was a high school junior and I only a freshman. "I wish you'd let me finish what I started to say."

"Go ahead," said Thelma. "That'll be the day when you don't have your say."

"I meant—I don't wanna get married."

"Never?"

"Maybe some day, but not right after college."

"You're sure planning ahead. You still got high school to finish."

"Ya gotta plan ahead, not just let things happen to ya. I wanna be somebody."

"Like what?"

I hesitated to tell her. Afraid she'd laugh at me.

"So whaddiya wanna be?"

"A writer," I whispered.

"A writer?" Thelma seemed disappointed in my choice. Then she perked up. "You wanna write for the movies?"

"No, I'd rather write stage plays."

"So why can'tja get married and still write? Anyway you'll change your mind when 'Mr. Fated-One' comes along."

"You and your 'Mr. Fated-One.' Hey, ya think Asher's your 'Mr. Fated-One?' "

Thelma shot me a baleful look. "It's none of your business who's my 'Fated-One.' "

"I was only kiddin'."

We had reached the entrance to the Prospect Avenue elevated station. Mr. Samuelson was there, as usual, handing out his business-type card with its saccharine message. "All is sweetness and light here and in the Hereafter."

A train pulled out of the station overhead causing the wooden platform to tremble. The three of us became striped with alternating bars of light and dark. Thelma and I walked on in silence. When the train's noise subsided, I said: "Your mom said somethin' funny when I was drinkin' the seltzer."

"What'chee say?"

"That love don't havta come before marriage. Sometimes it comes afta. Or even neva." I turned to face Thelma. "Were your mom and dad in love?"

"Before they got married? I dunno 'cause I wasn't here yet." Thelma giggled.

"Thelma Pearl!"

"Seriously. My parents were born and grew up in Poland. My mom was orphaned in a pogrom when she was maybe five years old. My Grandma took 'er in and groomed 'er to become a *rebbitzen* 'cause my Papa was studying to be a Rabbi. When he finished at the Vilna Yeshivah, he went off to America to find a position. He got one and sent for his mama and my mom. She was 17 and he was like 30 when they got married."

"Ya think they learned to love each other afterwards?"

Thelma rubbed her chin. "Guess so."

"I told your mom a lie: that my mama fell in love with my dad. See they got married through a matchmaker, so they probably weren't in love before. But, if you ask me, they still aren't."

"Why ya say that?"

"They have awful fights. Did your parents fight?"

"Not really. My mom useta yell sometimes, but my papa never raised his voice. Come to think of it . . . her screamin' stopped when my grandma got sick and came to live with us."

"Outa respect for the old lady?"

Thelma and I came to a standstill. As if she were thinking aloud, she said: "The yellin' useta be pretty regular."

"Like when she got 'the curse?' They say women get hysterical."

We began walking again. As if she were tracking a clue, Thelma rehashed the facts. "Moish and I useta share a room when we were kids. My parents slept in the other bedroom. The same time every month, Moish would go sleep with Papa and she'd take his bed. It was just before this switch that I'd be waked up by her hollerin'. I couldn't make out what she said 'cause they kept the door shut. The first night she'd come to sleep in my room, she'd lay in my brother's bed cryin' all night."

"So when your grandma came to live with ya?"

"We got the apartment we're in now with three bedrooms: one for my grandma, one for Papa and Moish, and one for Mom and me, right nexta Grandma's so we could hear if she needed somethin' in the middle of the night. But even afta Grandma died, Mom and I still shared the same bedroom. Moish moved into Grandma's room 'cause he was goin' to Yeshiva and needed a place to study."

"So whaddaya think?"

"I think I know what was goin' on."

"You do?" I stopped in my tracks and leaned toward Thelma.

Thelma grabbed my arm and propelled me ahead. She said nothing.

"Areya or ain'tcha gonna tell me?"

"Asher gave me a book to read. All about how a pious Jewish woman should behave. I flipped through it. On one page this sentence caught my eye: 'When a woman has her time, she is unclean.' "

"You mean your father made your mother sleep in another room 'cause she sme— It wasn't her fault; she couldn't take a bath during her period."

"No, silly. 'Unclean' means you can't have sex when a woman menstruates because it's dangerous. She has to go to the *mikveh* (through a ritual bath) to be purified. Then it's safe for them to do it again."

I whistled; that is, I tried to but no sound came out. "You know, Thel, that could explain— Well, somethin' happened once— " I fell silent. Debated with myself whether I should or should not tell her. "If I tell you, you have to swear that you won't breathe a word of it to no one. Not even to your mom."

Thelma kissed her pinky, placed it on her heart and lifted it heavenward.

"It happened about four years ago. My dad wasn't a travelin' salesman yet, so he was home more. My parents slept in what was supposed to be the dining room. It had French doors connectin' with the livin' room where I slept on a rollaway bed."

"So who slept in the bedroom?"

"A boarder."

"So get on with the story already."

"So don't interrupt. It musta been three in the morning. He useta come home pretty late."

"From work?"

"No. My dad said from playin' cards; my mom claimed he went to the *coorvas*."

Thelma's face appeared impassive as if she hadn't heard the word: "whores."

"My dad's hollerin' woke me. And my mom was sobbin'. I got out of bed, crept over to the French door, peeked through one of the glass panes. My dad was straddlin' her on the bed; he had her braid in his hand and was yankin' her head from side to side." I

68

turned away. "I don't think I oughta tell ya anymore."

"Aw, come on, Leah. That's not fair."

"I don't wanna remember it."

"You're afraid I won't keep my promise?"

I shook my head, "No."

"Leah, I won't tell a soul."

"Awright. Might as well finish what I started. My mom's cryin' and sayin' in Yiddish: 'One mustn't. Not when I've got the 'curse.' '"

"He shoulda known that."

"My dad doesn't believe in all that religious crap."

Thelma looked hurt.

"Well, that's what he calls it."

"So go on."

"He jerked her head back, pushed her down on the mattress, but she broke out of his grip, flung the French door open—it nearly hit me—and ran toward the bathroom. He came after her, but she'd locked herself in."

"Did he see you?"

"No. He was too mad to see straight. Kept poundin' his fists on the bathroom door and bellowin': 'You bitch. You bitch.' He went back to the bedroom, turned around and put a fist through one row of glass panes."

"Did you get cut?"

"No. While he was beatin' on the bathroom door, I jumped back in bed."

"Did your mom have'ta stay in the bathroom all night?"

"After she heard him snorin', she crept out, sat up all night in a livin' room chair. I never let on I heard or saw a thing. My mom thinks I could sleep through a fire."

We reached the corner where Thelma lived. "See ya." we said to each other.

I had two more blocks to go and two more hours before sunset. This stretch of the day of rest I disliked most; to sit in the gloom of the apartment waiting for the Evening Star to mark the end of the Sabbath. I let myself in; the long hallway was already tunnel-dark. As I neared the living room, my mom called to me in a choked voice: "Watch out for the glass on the floor." Just then my foot crunched some. My father must've been home!

"Are you all right?" I asked as I noted the two broken panes.

"We'll have supper as soon as *Shabbas* is out." She sat in the armchair positioned so she'd catch sight of the first star. I couldn't see her face.

It was a wretched evening. I sat opposite my mother at the oil-cloth-covered kitchen table and bent my head to my plate to avoid seeing her blackened left eye. I stayed at the table to do my Latin and picked at a pimple on my chin until it bled.

When I brought the rollaway bed into the middle of the room, Mama said: "You can sleep in the other twin bed. He won't be home anymore tonight."

I lowered one side of the bed and then the other, acting as if I hadn't heard her. She came over to help me with the sheet.

"I can do it by myself," I said and yanked it out of her hands. When I got into bed, I pulled the blanket between my legs, rammed it against my crotch and rocked myself to sleep.

Sometime during the night I dreamed I'm standing in front of Mme. Regina's salon. The bride wears only a slip. Her right arm is extended, a bouquet in hand. Suddenly she pitches the flowers through the plate glass window. There's no sound of glass breaking, but a round hole appears in the window. I duck for fear the hurtling bouquet will blacken my eye.

The groom rips off her slip, loops it around her neck like a noose. She tries to slap him. He seizes her arm, wrenches it from the shoulder socket. The hand falls to the floor, palm up. On it rests a small bible.

The bride grows taller and taller until her head scrapes the ceiling; her wig slips off. She snatches her arm back from the groom. Wielding it like a club, she stalks him. Through all of it, the set smile is fixed on her face. She gains on him; he crouches and grasps a free end of the slip. Tighter and tighter he tugs it around the bride's neck. She beats him with her arm, but many of the blows miss the mark. He draws the slip even tighter about her throat; a red stain darkens the white cloth. In a rage, the bride hurls her arm at the groom. It crashes through the plate glass window. Slivers of glass fall soundlessly to the sidewalk.

I must escape the arcing limb. I force myself awake.

Though still between waking and sleeping, I'm conscious of a warm ooze between my legs; a red stain soaking into the white sheet.

I wept, fear and joy flowing together in my tears. *I'm now your daughter, Eve.*

EXCESSES
Jean MacKellar

It was the custom, at the resort of Bresoles, to take a cup of the restorative waters twice a day. A dozen fountains gushed into a sparkling, vaporous pool at the far end of the glassed-in pavilion, and there, morning and afternoon, guests filled their cups. On canes, in wheel chairs, alone or clinging to the arms of green-smocked attendants, they made their way to the noisy, steaming pool for the water they would sip over the next hour, contemplating the health it would bring.

Some of the pilgrims seated themselves in the peacock-backed chairs that ranged around the walls, remaining in the pavilion to enjoy the warm, humid air and profit by the sight of those more or less ill than themselves. Others repaired to the benches outside, where they sat facing the sun. At noon they returned to their hotels and pensions for a lunch that was spartan or sumptuous, depending on how seriously they took their doctor's orders. In mid-afternoon they gathered again at the oval basin for a cup, which might be sipped during the hour-long concert at the white pergola by the pond.

Patrice Labatière stood in the great sunlit pavilion, scowling at the procession of health pilgrims come to take their morning prescription. Three days earlier he had survived a splendid smashup of his Porsche. His injuries were found to be not serious. However, since he had bruised his kidneys badly in another crash, his physician had recommended that he take a cure. He had been here for two days and was bored beyond words.

Sipping from his cup of now-lukewarm, faintly sulfurous water, Patrice felt nothing but disdain for the cure-seekers passing before him. None of them, he felt sure, had been in car wrecks such as he. They were here because they were old and infirm, neither of which had anything to do with him. It was a dismayingly lumpy, wrinkled collection of individuals on parade before his gaze. And he found the leaden routine almost beyond bearing.

When he checked into his hotel he'd been in such a state of shock still from the accident that he could hardly sign his name. Now, however, aside from the evidence on his face—the lacerations on his right cheekbone and his swollen eye—he almost wondered why he was here. Well, he had to admit to a general soreness throughout his body. He had promised to spend a week, although he feared that the tedium would make him genuinely ill.

There was only one redeeming feature to the place. At the Grand Hotel, where he was staying, one dressed for dinner, and at night the hotel's casino came to life. Then the seamed, flabby, over-weight, resigned personages of the days were for the most part replaced by a quite different crowd, which drove in from near and far to try their luck at Baccarat and roulette. These were gay and fashionable people, given to brandies and staying up all night, quite heedless of the lessons of excess which the daytime crowds at the fountain personified.

As Patrice gazed around the disheartening room, he found an unusual figure in one of the peacock chairs not far from where he stood. The woman was a glossy brunette—there was that, first of all, to distinguish her in this crowd where the heads ranged from iron grey to purest white—and she wore a crimson wool dress that could only be from the hand of a couturier. He guessed her age to be between 30 and 35.

With a dainty gesture, which might have been accompanied by a sigh, she reached for her white porcelain cup on the small table before her, and sipped moodily. This elegant creature, it was clear, was as bored as he.

In the distance trumpets seemed to sound. A design, as old yet as tonic as springtime, seemed to be set in motion. Adopting a bemused air, carrying his cup of water, Patrice began to stroll on a path that would take him past the brunette's chair. In spite of his stern concentration on the middle horizon, it was impossible for him not to be aware of how slim-hipped and long-limbed he was, what a different figure he cut from all the rest. At 24 years he was indisputably in his prime. Just in case she might not notice at once the damage to his face, he affected a light limp. Not enough to look crippled, but suggesting a topic of interest.

Choosing a chair not far from hers, he lowered himself gingerly into it and placed his cup on the wicker table nearby. His gaze swung, by chance it seemed, in her direction. The expression with which she was looking at him was open and friendly. It was the custom here to speak to people after encountering them several times. Gravely he nodded. She gave him a smile which was so natural and rueful that he found himself, without any compunction, rising again and going to sit in the chair beside her.

"*Bonjour, Madame,*" he said sincerely. He had noticed the heavy gold ring on her left hand with only a minor sense of disappointment. "Please excuse me for intruding on you like this, but I saw you sitting alone, and you were kind enough to smile at me in my loneliness . . . ."

She smiled even more at this. There was, in fact, a certain quizzical interest in her lovely, long-lashed eyes. He continued smoothly. "It's a lovely day, is it not? Not a day to be ill. I hope you aren't here for the same drab reasons as the rest of us." He made a gesture with his cup, gallantly lending his presence to the morose ranks of those who shuffled past them.

Actually, it was not correct to make an allusion to another's state of health here; this information was strictly voluntary. But the look that she gave his damaged cheekbone was so kind he found himself taking unusual liberties.

"Well!" she said with an informal little laugh which deprecated the lack of protocol in their beginning such a personal conversation. "Indeed, you aren't the sort one generally finds here!" But her manner did not reproach him. "I hope you're not suffering," she added, her gaze on his bruised eye.

A dark scab, several centimeters in breadth, had formed over the skin he'd lost when his cheekbone scrubbed the steering wheel. Patrice regretted the injury to his face at this moment because he had often been told that he looked very much like Alain Delon. A younger, slimmer version of Alain Delon. The same straight nose and fine brows, the same cobalt blue eyes, startling against his olive skin and dark wavy hair. This he wore in a romantic length, curling slightly on his collar. Nothing freaky, like so many of his age. For one thing, his father wouldn't have it, and besides, he himself felt he had certain responsibilities to his class. After all, his father was very rich. He owned a chain of distinguished furniture stores, and a lot of other things, besides.

Delighted that she had alluded to his injury, Patrice dismissed it with a wave of the hand. But then almost at once he began to tell her, in detail, about the accident. How it had happened in the Bois de Boulogne—he lived on the edge of the Bois and knew the area like the inside of his pocket—and how this idiot had emerged from a side road where no one had ever before emerged, and *voilà*. He had of course been going 75 kilometers an hour—a Porsche was not made to do less. But then he handled the crash with a sangfroid which only someone skilled in accidents could, spinning his wheel to take the impact on the car's right side instead of head-on. This was his sixth smashup, he admitted modestly; he now had a certain expertise.

"Just think!" his companion pronounced, her tone underlining the marvel of it. She settled back in her chair, crossing her legs with a pretty movement.

"I've had many serious injuries," he avowed. "But none of them were important." He touched his cheekbone. "This is nothing." It would not add to the esthetics of the conversation to mention his kidneys. "I really came here for the casino," he confessed. "Do you like to play?"

To his astonishment, her eyes, almost wicked in their amusement a moment before, clouded suddenly with tears.

"*He* liked to play," she said. "My husband. We came here every year to treat his gout. He had this madness for burgundy. You know how burgundy gives one gout."

"Everyone knows that burgundy gives one gout," Patrice agreed solemnly. "Even the most robust constitution." His finely-tuned ear had picked out at once that she spoke of her husband in the past tense.

"He would take the cure for two weeks, every spring, and in the evenings he played. I lost him in a sailing accident just two years ago."

"Two years ago!"

She nodded, producing a little handkerchief with which she

touched her eyes.

"But, Madame, that's already a very long time!"

"Not when you're sad," she answered, sniffing gently, pressing her nose.

"Grief is very sad, of course," he philosophised. "Still, it should not be taken to an extreme. You are so young, so charming, Madame. It seems to me like a dreadful waste . . . ." He did not actually touch her, but he leaned toward her chair, as if to protect her from such waste.

She looked at him encouragingly over the lace-trimmed hankie, waiting for him to go on.

"There's a saying . . . of course you know it already, so you won't be offended if I repeat it . . . 'Anything done to excess is in bad taste.' That means even good things. Even the best things. Burgundy. Sunshine." He gestured toward the sun pouring in the tall windows. "Health regimes . . . ." He glanced around at the people shuffling past, as if they were proof of the failure of health regimes. "Even love and devotion . . . even they can be overdone, you know."

She was smiling at him again now. "Anything done to excess is in bad taste," she repeated, considering. "I suppose. To be too honest . . . hmmm." She went on. "To be too sincere. . . . ."

"Exactly!" He caught up her litany. "To be too punctual. Too energetic . . . ."

"Too fashionable. Too . . . ."

"Virtuous," he proposed.

She frowned. Hastily, he regrouped. One could not go too fast. "Do you know the story of the Holy Man who ate only five olives a day?"

"Only five olives? No."

"One day a pilgrim came to him and said, 'Oh, Holy One, why do you eat exactly five olives each day?' And the Holy Man replied, 'Because seven would be too many and three would be pretentious.'"

She gave a delicious peal of laughter. It was exactly the response he had hoped for and seemed to him to hold great promise. Within a few moments they exchanged names. He asked her to have dinner with him, but she said she always ate dinner with an old couple she'd known for many years. She, too, was staying at the Grand Hotel. They would meet after dinner and go to the casino.

She was lovely in a gown of rose chiffon, which floated as she walked toward him. At the roulette table, her silky scarf occasionally slipped down one shoulder or the other, revealing the luscious curve of her bosom. She herself did not play, content to lean toward him as he matched the wheel, laughing when he won, pursing her lips with a little intake of breath when the numbers went against him.

A certain languorousness pervaded the room that night. It was exceptionally warm. Under the shaded light of the table, even the croupier's call, "Place your bets, ladies and gentlemen," followed by *"Rien ne va plus,"* as the ball began to click in the spinning wheel, had a certain indolence to it.

Patrice neither won so much that he became greedy for the game, nor did he lose enough to complain. At any other time he would have found it a boringly indecisive shifting about of luck. But on this night, it was the fragrant being at his side, more than the numbers on the black and red, that held his thoughts.

Toward eleven he was a handful of chips ahead when he gave her a nod which meant that this was all he intended to play. With an imperious gesture, he summoned a page to change the chips for him, then rewarded the man with a carelessly large tip.

The smile his lovely companion gave him was benign. Without a word she turned and led the way through the tall doors which gave onto the hotel's wide terrace. The gardens were starlit, the night mild. She moved to the carved stone balustrade, then stopped exactly at midpoint betwen two great flowering urns. Her silky scarf reflected gentle stirrings in the air as she stood there, rapt, a poem of femininity. When he came to her side, she turned to him, as he knew she would. Not a syllable passed between them. He gathered her into his arms.

She lifted her face. Her eyes seemed to contain dreams which only he could complete. He took his time. Slowly he brought his face down to hers. Her lips were parted, ready. The kiss he pressed upon them was over almost before it began. She made a movement of surprise, looked at him with wonder. Smiling tenderly he drew her closer. Now she was truly his. Expertly he brought his lips, half open, full upon hers.

She leaned against him. Her thighs pressed his. The fullness of her breasts branded him through his pleated evening shirt. The firmament whirled, oceans sank in on themselves, a private infinity stretched ahead. The kiss went on and on, in a life of its own, holding them together in its greedy clasp.

There was time, even, for Patrice to think. While one part of him reeled in rapture, another far corner of his mind had never been more alive and precise. This part of him was able to calculate to within a gnat's whisker the sequel to the kiss. He could foresee with almost boorish accuracy the number of steps that would be required for them to make their way back through the casino's tables, up the sweeping staircase, and down the royally-carpeted hallway to his own door. It was all there, unfolding before him. A moment of delay as the key did its job—the awkwardness cleverly concealed by another life-draining, hell-inspiring kiss—then into the room where the evening maid would have turned down the proud bed.

His luscious companion would gaze at him, drooping on his arm, as his fingers found the one or two fastenings of the diaphanous garments she wore. They would drop to the floor. Gently he would lay her in her dazzling nakedness across the bed. Still fully-clothed himself, he would proceed to minister to her loveliness with all the art that life had taught him. Soon she would be moved from a tender passivity to moans of responsiveness. Longings and beggings would pour from her exquisite little throat. Her head would toss on the lacy pillow. Unable to bear more, she would begin to tear off his clothing. His still white collar would be flung to perdition, his trousers kicked furiously to one side. Her trembling hands would be everywhere upon his splendid, taut body.

The fantasy did not need to go further; it was the facts which occupied him now. He would murmur a few words of endearment, the assurances so close to the feminine heart. Then he would give her another kiss—the kiss that would seal their fate and reduce the 200 steps ahead to no more than a shimmering of bird's wings.

"My angel," he whispered. "Oh, my loveliest of angels . . . ."

Her pale face was turned up to him. The expression in it was not that of the dainty widow, near tears. Nor was it the apt companion who laughed when he won and pouted when he lost at the gaming table. Perhaps it was the glint of a distant star that was reflected in this new look in her eyes. Her lips, still sweetly full from the kiss, curved in a smile which he could not fathom, as she spoke.

A moment later, her scarf trailing her scent, she was moving quickly across the flagstones of the terrace toward the lights of the great room beyond. His arms were empty. She had said something which he had not heard then, but which he replayed now from the echo in his mind.

"Anything more, my divine young man, truly, would be in bad taste."

GREEN RIBBONS
Clay Fulghum

"Durn cat," Mrs. Flowers grumbled and threw her back-scratcher at the striped feline that was meowing at the foot of the bed.

The backscratcher missed its target, and the cat meowed again.

"I'm gonna get you someday, cat," she threatened. "You jus' sit there like you own the place. But what'd you do—didn't I cook those chicken necks and rice?"

The animal regarded her with mild eyes.

Mrs. Flowers' dogs, housed in the adjacent room, heard that their mistress was awake and were whimpering loudly. Baby Pup was barking every now and then in his sharp stacatto.

"I'm coming, Baby!" Mrs. Flowers yelled. "And you, Blackie, shut up! I'm getting there as fast as I can."

She took two pain killers, like she had done every morning since the cold weather came, and tried to sit up. But her arms and shoulders hurt too much to support her.

"Hmmp. I'm worse than I was yesterday," she thought out loud. "Those dogs got a better lot than me by far. I'll always take Blackie out to the vet's in a cab if I have to and pay for it outa the grocery money. But who I got gonna see about me?" Her husband, Cal, had died several years before, and she had never had children. The doctor had said that despite her fine size and robust health, it would be unwise. She never did quite understand.

Mrs. Flowers turned onto her side with difficulty, smoothed the worn army blanket, and looked out the window at the althea bush, bare now, and the tangle of devil vines and kudzu that was trying to take over the yard. The sky was bleak, and a drizzle had set in. She was slowly realizing that it would be one of the bad days, with movement severely limited. She might even have to call Ruth or another neighbor to bring over a hamburger from the stand down the street, if she couldn't make it to the kitchen.

"Oh," she exclaimed, as soon as she thought of Ruth. "How could I have forgot! Ruth supposed to come over here today anyway. I won't have to make no phone calls to nobody about helping me out. Ruth gon' be here!"

Mrs. Flowers had helped deliver Ruth nearly nineteen years ago, and had watched her grow up—a totally uneventful childhood. Now Ruth had a job two days a week as a scrub nurse in the hospital, and before her shift, she would drop by to see if Mrs. Flowers was still living or not.

"And it's almost time for her right now," Mrs. Flowers noticed, relieved. "She better have brought that extra key I gave her."

Mrs. Flowers picked up her mirror from the table next to the bed and began to comb her hair in preparation. As always, the face she saw made her shudder a little. For the crepey dry skin with its brown age marks had once been clear and smooth and white, and she had never quite adjusted to the change. Her eyes were the same, though, startlingly green, and fiery, too, when she got mad.

She arranged her short gray hair so that the bald spot would be concealed, and buttoned the sleeves of her faded nightgown.

"If only I had put my lipstick where I could reach it, I wouldn't look so ugly," she fumed.

In a few minutes the doorbell rang, and Mrs. Flowers hollered for Ruth to come in. She heard some fumbling and the familiar shuffle across the old linoleum floor in the living room. Then, there was Ruth, her colorless eyes taking in the room critically, evaluating for the umpteenth time the yellowing wallpaper, the ancient pictures of Jesus tacked above the dresser, the little bedside table with the lamp on it that Mrs. Flowers never turned off.

"Stop gawking and come on in here," Mrs. Flowers said, a little irritated. There were things to do.

Ruth gave a sidewise glance and entered. "You sure do look awful," she offered by way of greeting.

"Okay now, Ruth, don't start like that. Take off your raincoat and have a seat." There was a note of pleading in Mrs. Flowers' voice now. The girl was so touchy these days.

Ruth threw the raincoat across a straight-backed chair and

pulled the chair up to the bed. Then she sat down and carefully crossed her legs, shapeless as posts, at the ankles. Her damp, limp hair clung to her cheeks.

"I'm gonna ask you again, why'd you ever buy those rose bushes," she said in an accusatory tone. "You knowed Anna Nora would steal 'em. I told you she was worse than ever." A gleam appeared in her eyes that animated her face a trifle. Mrs. Flowers frowned and her brows came together. "You don't mean ...?" she ventured.

"Yes, I do," Ruth snapped. "She's gone and dug 'em up. What else could you expect? They sittin' in her front yard."

Mrs. Flowers forgot for a moment her pleasure at having company, forgot the chores she needed Ruth to do, forgot even her pain. She had bought two rose bushes on her last trip out over a month ago and had paid a child a dollar to plant them after dark so Anna Nora wouldn't see.

"Here, honey," Mrs. Flowers cajoled. "You help me outa this bed. I'm gonna go over there and pull 'em right back up!"

Ruth reluctantly gave the old woman her big peasant hands and Mrs. Flowers sat upright, then maneuvered her great bulk until she was standing. Her knees seemed to have grown to twice their normal size during the night and a deep piercing pain criss-crossed her back. She realized that she couldn't straighten her-self and that she was too weak to walk very far. But they started in the direction of the front door anyway, the heavy older woman leaning on the younger one's arm. It was hard going.

"What's happening to me?" Mrs. Flowers wondered. "I should start taking that heart medicine again, I guess." A dark thought formed in the back of her mind, that she didn't give voice. Ruth had begun talking about Harvey Ratchett and wouldn't listen anyway.

"Have you heard what he's doing now?" she was asking.

Mrs. Flowers nodded noncommitally. It was all she could do to put one foot in front of the other, and Ruth was expecting her to pay attention to that palaver. Besides, didn't she know that Harvey would never give her a second thought? She looked and acted like she was thirty. And Harvey probably had his choice of girls, despite his peculiar habits and turn of mind. He'd inherited his mother's black eyes. That was enough.

"After he left Atlanta," Ruth said, "he hitchhiked all the way down to Tallahassee. That's where his folks were born, you know."

Mrs. Flowers stopped to rest. "Ruth," she said, and her eyes flashed, "I know all there is to know about Harvey's 'folks'."

Ruth continued. "He had good luck there in Tallahassee. He met three other Ratchetts. He says he's gonna visit every Ratchett in the whole state." She smiled, distorting her features. "He's using telephone directories to track 'em down."

They were nearly at the front door now and Mrs. Flowers was having trouble breathing. "Honey," she said. "Now you just shut up about that fool Harvey. Just shut up, you hear?" There was a strident note in her voice. "Can't you see how bad I'm hurting? It's gonna be all I can do to get back in bed. Here, you feed the dogs. You aren't any help to me walkin' noways. I'm gonna hold onto the furniture and go back and lie down—if I can. I can't worry about no rose bushes now!"

Ruth stamped away, her lips stuck out.

"I knew I been goin' downhill," Mrs. Flowers thought frantically, "but I figured I had more time. What'll happen to the dogs?"

With energy born of determination, she made it to the bed and heaved herself onto it, breathing hard, and reaching into the drawer of the table fumbled around until she found her nitroglycerin tablets. She took four—twice the prescribed dose—and in a minute started to feel better.

She banished the dark thought with an act of the will.

Ruth came back into the room and announced in an arch manner that she had to leave.

"Ruthie, I didn't mean to speak rough," Mrs. Flowers said in a conciliatory tone. "You know how much I like you comin' to visit."

Ruth paid no attention, though, and snatched up her raincoat silently. She gave only a brief goodbye nod.

When the door slammed, Mrs. Flowers sighed. She hadn't meant to offend. It was just that talk about the Ratchetts always riled her up. There were too many memories. "And Ruth," she thought, "why that girl can't think of anything else but Harvey—and that mother of his, ol' Lilly Jane, with her hifalutin airs."

She recalled the time she had cornered Lilly Jane in one of the storerooms at the mill, and Lilly Jane had shown her true stripe, kicking wildly and screaming more loudly than even Mrs. Flowers.

"I got in a good lick or two that day," she chuckled grimly. "And Cal never run after her no more either, after he seen what them long fingernails done to my face." There were still two small scars.

In the midst of such thoughts, Mrs. Flowers went to sleep. She hadn't intended to. But sleep had become irresistible lately. In fact it was actually shortening her days so that less and less seemed to be happening in the world.

When the telephone rang—much later—she awakened with a start, disoriented and scared. She had no idea how much time had passed. Her watch had run down and the sky remained overcast like it had been all day. Only the cold evening dampness sweeping through the cracks in the windows gave hint that night was coming on.

The telephone kept on ringing. Mrs. Flowers reached for the receiver, heavy and unwieldy. The pain had returned, with a vengeance.

When she finally got the receiver off the hook and to her ear, she found Jonnie Davis on the other end, the woman she paid to do her shopping every two weeks.

"What you planning to do about those newspapers in your front yard?" Jonnie asked her right off. "We got enough trouble with those worthless new mill people moving in here, dumping their boxes and stuff every which-a-place. They gonna pull this neighborhood down lower'n it is already, and that'll be a heap low. Why, I saw an old sofa bed in the ditch just yesterday. Next...."

But Mrs. Flowers stopped her. For something in Jonnie's tone had triggered a deep hurt that was not to be denied—even now.

"Look here, Jonnie," she gasped. It was difficult to form words. "This may be the bummest house on the block, but the mill give it to me. Don't you go throwin' off on the mill and mill people when the likes of you set home and don't even try to find no job! I'll see to those papers soon enough. Don't you worry about it none!"

Mrs. Flowers had worked at the mill most of her life. When she was seven she had helped with rush orders. At fourteen, her mother had taken her out of school to work full-time. She knew there were a lot of sorry mill people. But to hear a low-rent type like Jonnie say it!

The outburst exhausted her, however, and she felt pain radiating down her left arm. The room and all the objects in it were blurring around the edges.

Jonnie, ignoring the rebuff, proceeded with the real reason for her call. "Forget about them papers," she said. "I got something else to tell you. A piece of real bad news."

Mrs. Flowers' hands grew suddenly clammy.

"Your niece's been killed—the one that lives across the river." Jonnie managed a respectful silence.

"Murdered," she went on, "and they don't know who. He done her in with a jar of pineapple preserves. She just finished puttin' 'em up."

Mrs. Flowers didn't respond. She simply registered the information.

"Oh Lord forgive," she thought. "Lord forgive. I should be glad that nothing like that happened to me. I deserved it more'n she ever did, and her still young. Oh Lord forgive. I been lucky in my life. So lucky."

She let the telephone drop to the floor with a clatter, and after a while Jonnie's harsh exclamations and inquiries ceased.

"Lord forgive me," Mrs. Flowers' mind was saying, "I know I been bad. I know I done a lot of hellin'." Then she didn't even seem to be thinking in words at all. There was a black funnel around her and only she was stationary. Her consciousness was unclear, or rather clear but in a different kind of way. She was remembering how her life used to be, and there were images and sequences of images imposed upon the black funnel. She was remembering how it was when she was with Cal in bed, how her body moved, straining, stretching, and raising up to get the most pleasure possible. Her hair had been a deep auburn then, thick and ropy. He would hurt her sometimes, pulling it, winding it around his hands. Those were the good days when Cal was working at the mill, too, and the great machines were weaving silk. What a sight it was to look up and see multicolored waves of cloth suspended in air with the sunshine from the skylight filtering through them. She used to take some of the odds and ends home with her and make pillow cases out of them, out of rose and aquamarine and fuchsia silk. On Saturday night she would put a green silk ribbon in her hair and slyly observe the men's faces light up when they saw her. Cal would always be watching jealously.

But the colors were swirling now too, dissolving, and losing their brightness.

"Oh God!" Mrs. Flowers cried.

The cat, which had not stirred for hours, came walking toward her, curious.

Outside it was dark.

THE SILVER BRACELET
Roselore Fox

Karlsruhe, November 1939. I was six years old.

Through the half-open window drifted the cold winter wind and with it the dull, steady rhythm of boots pounding the asphalt beneath them. Loudspeakers blared marching songs. Germany was at war.

"Where are the soldiers going, Papa?"

Father had been listening to the radio. He turned the volume down and walked toward me. "They're being sent to the front, Ursula."

"What's a front, Papa?"

He frowned at me, his lips parted as if to answer my question. "Go help Liesl in the kitchen," he said instead.

Liesl was busy washing the floor. She lifted me on to the table. "Stay out of the water," she grumbled.

I sat stiff and uncomfortable on the edge of the table, careful not to wrinkle the cloth she had starched and ironed the night before.

"What's a front, Liesl?" I asked.

Liesl came right to the point. "That's where they shoot bullets at people," she said and clasping her hand over her mouth, she apologized. "I shouldn't have told you that."

"Is it safe to let the children walk in the streets now?" I heard Liesl ask Father when I got ready for school.

"For the time being," he replied and walked to the window. There was a faint rumbling far in the distance.

"That's French artillery," Liesl explained, "but don't worry, they're too far away."

As usual, Miriam waited for me on the corner.

"Why don't you ever come to my house, Miriam?"

She shook her head. "Mother says not to."

"You never showed me where you live."

Miriam didn't answer. She danced gracefully away from me. Like a small ballerina, she lifted her skirt, her toes barely touching the sidewalk.

"I'll dance on the stage when I'm older," she said, fluttering long silken eyelashes at me and I knew I would go to see her, admire her, attend each one of her performances.

At school we shared the same bench. We ate our *Vesper* together, and sometimes we would trade our food. Miriam's lunch always tasted better than mine.

"Why don't you have a mother, Ursel?" she asked me one day.

"She died," I said miserably, hating her for bringing up the subject. She and all the other children had mothers. I still missed mine terribly.

"I have Liesl," I said quickly.

"She's just your housekeeper. That's not the same." Miriam frowned and took a large bite from the apple I was trying to save for the walk home after school.

"I know and I don't really like her," I said, "but then I have someone besides Liesl."

"You do? Who is it?"

"Frau Weissblum. She's almost as nice as my mother."

Miriam lifted one eyebrow. She seemed surprised. "The lady who lives in your building?"

"She's my very best friend," I nodded and hoped Miriam would be duly impressed.

Perhaps Miriam hadn't heard. She seemed puzzled. "Frau Weissblum still lives there?"

It was an odd question. I didn't know what she meant. I wanted to ask, but she had closed her eyes. Suddenly she lifted her arms. Her fingertips touched over her head. Balancing on her toes, she executed a graceful pirouette.

I was fascinated. "I'll come to see you every night. I'll even bring you flowers when you dance on the stage," I said, aching inside, wanting to be as beautiful and graceful as she was.

She mocked me. "'I'll bring you flowers.'...Only men bring flowers to a star." Long, silky lashes fluttered and teased. "And they'll bring me diamonds and pearls," she whispered, bowing to an invisible audience.

I was embarrassed. I hadn't known. But Miriam would be famous. I had to think of something to please her. "I'll invite you for tea then . . .," I said. Frau Weissblum always asked me to come and have tea. Miriam would like that—at least I hoped she would.

She curtsied. "Tea will be fine, *gnädige Frau.*"

We bought ice cream on the corner where the fountain played an endless game of rising into the air and then falling like a shower of diamonds back into its ornate basin. And happy to be together, we watched the pigeons bob their heads eagerly for the crumbs we spread on the ground. Her long curly hair flowed in the wind and for a moment completely covered her face.

"I could tell you a secret," she said from behind that curtain of curls.

I loved secrets. "Why don't you tell me?"

She whisked the hair away from her eyes. "I can't," she said and spreading her arms for balance she danced on the edge around the circle of the fountain.

The next morning she was absent from school. I asked the teacher if she was ill. He pretended he hadn't heard. I tugged his sleeve. "Where is Miriam, Herr Daneker?"

He seemed annoyed with me. "She's not coming back," he said and went back to his desk. I followed him.

"Did Miriam move away?"

He shrugged his shoulders and didn't answer me. I stood on my toes to see his face, but he looked away.

"But Miriam is my friend," I cried.

"You should choose your friends more carefully," he said loud enough for the others to hear and I was ashamed and confused but I didn't know why.

"Frau Weissblum is leaving," Liesl informed me a few days later.

I asked where she was going. There was no answer.

"How long will she stay?"

Father stood in the doorway. He had been listening. "Liesl,

you . . .," he said sharply, but didn't finish the sentence.

I decided to ask her myself.

"Dr. Weissblum" read the polished brass plate on the heavy door. I had asked my father about the title.

"She's a doctor of philosophy," he explained.

"What's philosophy?" I asked.

He pondered my question for a moment. "Philosophy is the search for wisdom and truth, Ursula. It's a science," he added.

"What's a science, Papa?"

He moaned. "Go help Liesl in the kitchen."

Frau Weissblum was not very tall and perhaps just a bit heavy. But to me she was perfect. Her smile was warm and one could watch it play on her lips and then slowly spread over her face to her eyes. And it would stay there all during my visits. It made me feel comfortable and welcome. Her hands were soft and white and her fingers wre covered with exquisite rings. Her nails were long and buffed to a soft, shimmering glow. And she wore long strands of pearls. Sometimes, when she hugged me, the pearls would get tangled with the giant silk bow I wore in my hair.

I had visited Dr. Weissblum every day for almost two years. Liesl was wrong; Frau Weissblum couldn't possibly leave. I'd ring the bell and it would take just a second or two for her to open the door. She would smile and gather me up in her arms, and I knew she had been waiting for me. We would brew the tea in a large, silver samovar. She served fresh, delicate pastries on a platter lined with lacy napkins. Sometimes she had *Marcipan*, covered with chocolate or powdered sugar and it was terribly difficult to eventually say, "*Nein, danke schön*, Frau Weissblum," and really mean it.

On warm summer days we took our cups and the pastries out to the veranda. The samovar gleamed in the afternoon sunlight and I'd look at my reflection in the strange silver teapot. My face appeared distorted and funny. Frau Weissblum put her cheek next to mine and our faces would blend into one image. Hugging each other, we'd giggle and have a wonderful time.

I could not imagine why she would leave. My fingers caressed the plate with her name. Then I rang the bell.

It took her a long time before she came to the door. Instead of the smile there was a frown on her face.

90

Her *"Guten Tag,* Ursula," didn't sound like she was happy to see me. Two empty suitcases lay on the floor.

I held out my arms and when she cupped my face with her hands, I saw she didn't wear any rings.

"I'll make tea for you," she said quietly, and I went to the veranda to wait.

A few minutes later she brought the samovar and two cups. Wanting to help, I went to the kitchen for sugar.

"I don't have any pastries for you," she apologized when I came back.

"See my face?" I said desperately, wanting her to put her cheek next to mine, wanting her to laugh with me at the reflection in the teapot, but she didn't hear me. Or was she ignoring me? She couldn't go away; I needed her too much. Should I tell her that at times I made believe she was my mother?

My heart pounded. Should I go home now? But then I wouldn't know. I played with the bow in my hair, then straightened my dress. Not knowing what else to do, I unfolded my napkin and then folded it again.

Suddenly I found myself talking very fast. "Are you really going away? Liesl told me you're leaving and I think Father got angry with her. I hope it isn't true. Because I will miss you very much." And now I felt terribly unsure of myself, because she was not looking at me, would not talk to me. Was she angry with me? Was it possible that we were no longer friends?

She rose abruptly. "I have to dress, Ursula," she said, but I ran after her.

"If you're going away then I'd like to say goodbye to you," I said indignantly. She turned to look at me. There was a smile, but not in her eyes. This one was only on her lips.

"Come with me," she said and took me to the living room. The thick Persian rugs lay rolled together in a corner. The paintings had been taken off the walls, cardboard boxes were strewn across the floor. She saw my surprise and shrugged.

"I don't even know why I bothered ...."

She opened one of the drawers of the mahogony chest and reached inside. Extracting a small box, she removed the lid as if to check the contents and then put it into the pocket of her skirt.

"You have to go now," she said without looking at me, and

taking my hand, she walked me into the hall. Her eyes were closed when she hugged me. Then she pressed the package into my hand.

"That's for you," she whispered. The door closed. I was still standing there, when it opened again.

She reached for me. Her cheek was wet when it touched mine. *"Blagaslovy tebya bog,* Ursula," she whispered, and then, her voice suddenly harsh, she said, "Go on home now."

When I got to my room I opened the package. It contained a row of small, silver coins. They were tarnished, almost black, but artfully arranged into a bracelet. One coin half covered the next, much like the scales of a fish. It was simple, unpretentious but very beautiful.

Father called the coins *Kopeken.* They were from Russia, he said, and told me to take good care of them.

I tried very hard to remember what it was Frau Weissblum had said to me, but the strange words had slipped my mind.

"Did your doctor friend tell you where she's going?" Liesl asked, but Father interrupted her and said it was time to start dinner.

When I rang Frau Weissblum's doorbell the next day, there was no one to answer. The small brass plate with her name had been removed, leaving a bare rectangular spot on the door. In its place was a strange looking star, two awkwardly placed triangles carved into the beautiful wood with a sharp knife or a screwdriver.

Father kept the bracelet for me for many years. "Don't wear it like this," he warned. "The clasp is thin and worn. You might lose it."

Eventually a jeweler repaired it—or at least said he did.

It was 1949. I was on the Neckar River near Stuttgart. I had rented a *Kajack.* It was a warm, incredibly beautiful day. Farther back, I had passed an angler sitting on his heels. He had waved to me. Now I had the river all to myself. I drifted, enjoying the sun. I glanced at my watch. It was getting late. My left hand extended skyward, the right pushing the paddle hard with a powerful backward stroke. I felt the bracelet open and watched helplessly as it slid from my arm into the water.

I sat motionless for a long time, watching the last ripples fade into nothingness.

I saw my reflection in the smooth, shimmering surface of the water and for a fleeting moment there was another face next to mine. Then the images blended with the motions of the river.

"Blagaslovy tebya bog...."

I called my father on my way home. "Do you know what it means?"

He thought for a moment. "That's Russian for 'May God protect you.' Where did you hear that?"

I didn't answer. Too many years had passed. And her words belonged to me.

OLD GLORY
Bruce Kaiper

At exactly zero eight hundred Mike Spolecki unfurled Old Glory. With a fifteen foot hoist and a twenty-nine foot fly, it was the largest flag in San Francisco's financial district. Mike's brain child. Kept the old Pacific American Building visible. In the news.

Using a plastic tarp for an under cloth, he unrolled the folded banner lengthwise across the tar-coated roof. He disliked doing it this way—touching the ground violated military custom. But the swirling Market Street winds might yank it from his hands or drag him with it over the side. Adverse publicity would destroy Pacific American's frail reputation: "Patriotic Security Guard Falls to his Death for Old Glory." All the queers and peace creeps would howl. So he played it safe and kept the banner in thirds until he'd run it up the flagstaff.

The encircling stainless steel and glass towers were dazzling in the morning light. For how much longer would visitors to the city be able to see his flag? Banks, insurance companies, international conglomerates, all flexed their muscles on Market Street, squeezing out the older captains of commerce. Pacific American lacked the cold, heady appearance of its younger neighbors. Eighteen-storied and squat, it had the cracked granite face of a drill sergeant. When its boilers broke down or its elevators stopped working, he could curse it, kick it, knowing it would snap back to life. Only last year he could still see its scroll-lined cornices from Embarcadero Freeway; his flag waved proudly in a channel of air. But cranes and steel girders were filling that space, closing the last door to the Bay's fresh breeze. What good was a flag that couldn't be seen?

Mike dragged the tarp up to the flagstaff and untied the hoisting cable. He had enjoyed raising the flag for twenty-eight years and wouldn't stop now. Besides today his boy would earn the respect of his nation and the flag would honor his deeds. Little Stevie, a Marine. Mike grinned. His youngest son, the one he'd predicted wouldn't amount to anything, had become another Audie Murphy. Medal of Honor. Presidential Unit Citation. Vietnam Presidential Unit Citation. Rose to a commanding officer while the other grunts shot dope into their veins.

"My boy!" Mike shouted at distant executives behind the shimmering glass. "A Marine!"

Then he bent his knees, gripped a hem of the flag with one hand and quickly pulled it up so a grommet could slip onto a cable hook. Air swept under the cloth, billowing it as he hoisted it up the pole. A cable pulley rang against the steel. Each fastened grommet made the flag tougher to hold; it snapped and writhed like a flying serpent. But Mike wrapped a leg around the flagstaff and hoisted Old Glory to the top, whistling "To the Colors" through his teeth.

"Who you shoutin' at, Spolecki?"

Otis Payne ambled out of the stairwell, chewing a mangled stogie, and gave Mike a lopsided smile.

"Thought the Stars and Stripes finally pulled you off the roof, you were yellin' so loud. Was that your kid's name I heard?"

Mike nodded, but kept whistling and watching the flag slap the breeze.

"Shit. This ain't boot camp. You're too old to be playin' soldier. The only thing guys like us can do for our country is rest peaceful in the Presidio under a marble slab."

How did Payne ever survive Korea? Mike wondered. Claimed he had fought in an all black company on Heartbreak Hill. Claimed he'd been another Cab Calloway until a mortar shell rearranged his face. Mortar shell! Drinking hootch probably had done that. If Payne had enlisted in the Marines, they would've kept him off the front lines so as not to encourage the enemy.

"Aren't you supposed to be in the lobby, Payne? It's zero eight twelve."

"Zero eight twelve. Shit." Payne spit a glob of tobacco juice on the tar. "Your kid just called."

"Steve?"

"Nope. Doug. Says he'll meet you in front of the Ferry

Building at noon for a talk. Sounded uptight."

Mike fastened the cable to the flagstaff and began rolling up the tarp.

"He's worried about Steve, I guess."

"What about 'im? That commando team of his tryin' to topple a dictator or somethin'?"

"They don't topple nothing, Payne. They're a peace-keeping force. They fight terrorists."

"It's hard to know who is and who ain't these days, Spolecki."

Mike carried the tarp into the air-cooling shed and laid it beside the mixing chambers. Explaining details to Payne was aggravating. The man was cynical; he'd twist the simplest fact into its opposite.

"Where's he stationed?" Payne asked when Mike had locked the door. "Or is that top secret?"

"Nevada, last I heard. He could be anywhere right now. A Marine buddy of his called Doug two nights ago and said we should keep our eyes on the news. Steve's involved in something big. Should happen today."

"Yeah, I'll do that, Spolecki. This town needs a few heroes." He bit the end off his stogie and shoved what remained into his coat pocket as he sauntered to the stairs.

"Oh, and Payne! Keep this to yourself . . .for security reasons."

"Security? Shit, Spolecki. Any two-bit spy in Frisco could guess what's happenin' just listenin' to you brag."

Twelve ten. Mike scanned the Chronicle's feature section as he hurried down Market Street. "President says guerilla terror must end in El Salvador." "Libya claims American hostages are C.I.A.." Steve's task force was needed everywhere.

Excitement raced through Mike's body. What a responsibility for a few men to assume: handpicked by the top brass to penetrate enemy territory in order to rescue lives. Crackerjack specialists surviving by wits alone. No backup protection. Wars were fought differently these days. Commandos. Special Forces. When he had been a Marine, countries were invaded by whole armies. Soldiers never fought alone. Iwo Jima had been his toughest battle. Thousands had died. But when that ragged flag lashed to a pipe rose on Mount Suribachi thousands more had cheered. Who would ever cheer his son? Would he remain unknown?

Doug was waiting for him on a bench in the Ferry Building's shadows; he too was reading a newspaper. Casually dressed in a sport coat and slacks, he looked younger than his thirty six years; yet the bright sparks that once glowed in his eyes like polished brass buttons had vanished. One stint in Vietnam had made him sullen, reserved. The Marines offered him a well-paid commission and he turned them down. Doug should've been where his brother was now. He still had the square shoulders and tapered waist of an officer. The lean bone face. But he chose business. Typewriter sales. Why did a man of his caliber pick that for a living?

"I think Steve's in Libya, Pop. If they had him in Nevada, they must've been training him for desert conditions."

"Are you sure?" Mike asked, sitting beside him.

Doug wrinkled his brow and nodded. "It's only a guess. But the President has warned Libya enough about our hostages. Negotiations have broken off. He's gotta act now or lose public support. It's the Iranian thing all over again. Don't you see?"

The kid's a born strategist, Mike thought. A quick, military-type mind.

"But they'll never get our hostages out of Tripoli, Pop, no matter how many helicopters they use. It's suicidal." His voice cracked with the word. "One technical error and it's over."

The sudden pessimism stung Mike deeply. He searched his son's face for some sign of apology or guilt for making such a statement. Had Doug lost faith in his brother? In the Marines? Suicidal? That was coward's talk. What had happened to Doug in Vietnam? He had been one of the fortunate ones: he'd survived Khe Sanh, won combat ribbons, had no noticeable scars. But his fighting spirit was gone. Doug was abandoning Steve when Steve needed him most.

"You're wrong, son. Steve's gonna make it. Tripoli's old stomping ground for the Marines. They can't lose."

"We said that in Vietnam, Pop."

Doug recounted the Iranian rescue mission that had failed. He criticized the government's efforts at diplomacy. "We're not white knights, Pop. The Marines can't invade any country and expect people to throw flowers...."

97

But the Marine Hymn gradually swelled in Mike's head, driving out his son's sour notes. He gazed up under the Embarcadero overpass at his distant flag waving proudly over Market Street. He alone would cheer for Steve.

Seventeen fifty. Mike rode the bus to his Pacific Heights flat thinking only of Steve. No word of the mission in the afternoon papers. People went about their daily business unaware of history being made. Had the rescue team struck yet? It was probably early morning in Libya, if that's where Steve was. Sand. Camels. Olive trees. Mike knew very little about the place. Letty would have searched through her National Geographics for the pertinent facts. She would have been proud of her boy; he favored her. But Mike had sold the Geographics after her death. How was he to know he'd need them today?

When he got home he turned on both the T.V. and radio news. The neighbors would bang on the ceiling, but he didn't care. They would soon be proud to have a national hero's dad living above them.

Twenty fifteen. The prime time programs had started: sitcoms, cop shows, and cable channel movies. Mike sipped coffee to stay awake and occasionally stepped out on the balcony to watch the Pacific fog roll in. Rain tomorrow. Too bad. He so wanted to fly the flag in celebration.

Twenty two hundred. He called Doug. Maybe he had heard reports on the F.M. stations. Nothing except that the President had reaffirmed his pledge to the hostages' families; he'd bring them home diplomatically or otherwise. Perhaps Doug's guess was wrong. Would the President make public pronouncements while commandos raided Tripoli? Mike felt weary and increasingly sad. Maybe his son hadn't gone after all. He might be sitting in an American barracks that very moment wishing that he hadn't alerted the family.

"It's out of your hands, Steve," Mike said to his son's color photograph on the coffee table. "Your job is to obey. You've done enough for your country. More than your dad or your brother." Then he settled in his soft chair and let the T.V. lull him to sleep.

The abrupt end of canned laughter woke him. A familiar voice had entered the room: the President of the United States. What time was it? Zero one hundred. A new morning. The President's face was haggard and pale; the highly-polished veneer had cracked. He was somberly reading from a prepared statement beneath the official seal.

"It was a bold plan conceived by myself to free our hostages; a historic attempt to preserve American liberty and the rights of our citizens. I and I alone assume full blame and total responsibility. Good night."

That was all? Had Mike slept through most of the President's statement? He rushed to the phone to call Doug. But it started ringing as he clasped the receiver.

"I'm sorry, Pop," a weak, almost strange voice whispered on the other end. "I'll be right over."

His son hung up before he could reply. Mike returned to his chair. Keep calm, he told himself. Steve is all right. Steve's a survivor. Why were Mike's hands trembling so? A news commentator summarized what had happened to the rescue team using maps of Libya and wire photos of poor quality. Helicopter wreckage. Charred bodies. Was Steve alive or dead? Had he escaped? No names of soldiers were mentioned. Statistics of fatalities, wounded, captured, and escaped collided, then faded in his brain.

Doug silently entered the apartment and stood beside him as the story unfolded. The task force had landed on a secret air strip in the Red Desert, within striking range of Tripoli, only to have been surprised by waiting Bedawi soldiers. Leaks in the operation, the newsman said; the Libyan high command had been warned. Had others besides Steve sent messages to their families that agents intercepted? Mike wondered. Had other proud parents bragged prematurely about their sons?

Then an Associated Press photo flashed on the screen showing hideous corpses smoldering on the hot desert sand and Arab soldiers poking them with sticks.

"The bastards!" Doug cried out. He kicked the T.V. set, exploding its video images into blinking dots and hissing lines. "The rescue was stupid. I told you, Pop. Didn't I? The President didn't give a damn about our guys. He used them. Steve shouldn't 've volunteered."

"Don't, Doug." Mike rose from his seat and twisted the reception knob.

"But Steve's caught in that hell hole. He can't escape. He might be dead..."

"Don't!" Mike's hand struck his son's cheek before he could stop it. The blow stung his fingertips. "Not now," he whispered. "Not in this house."

Theirs had been a Marine family, two generations of fighters, never touched directly by death until... Now their bravest member was missing in action, in need of help. Arguing the mistakes of a battle wouldn't bring him home. They had to be with Steve in their thoughts, fight by his side, carry him if need be to safety. A Marine would do no less.

Early the next morning the Marines confirmed Steve's death. Doug sat in the kitchen, watching the drumming rainfall. But Mike went to work. The morning *Chronicle* had a photo of a charred soldier on its front page. Bewildered bus passengers stared at it in silence.

Payne met him in the lobby and suggested he return home. Instead Mike went to Pacific American's roof. He'd fly the flag half-mast—a fitting tribute to his boy. To hell with the military's bad weather rules. Old Glory had to be seen.

Gusts of rain pummeled the banner as he unfolded it on the roof. Wind whipped his face and twisted the stripes. Undaunted, Mike wrestled the giant banner to the flagstaff. Anchoring both feet on the slippery roof, he pulled the first grommet to the cable hook. A blast of wind hit his back and lifted the flag skyward, pushing him with it toward the roof's edge. The wind unfurled the flag to its full length and it flapped and whirled above the Pacific American sidewalk. Wet patrons were huddled within the entryway of Wells Fargo, waiting for the doors to open. Should Mike call for help? Would they hear him?

"Let it go!" they would shout. "Don't be a fool!" He couldn't let go. He had to win this tug of war. But could he hold on much longer? His fingers were cramping. He pulled with all his strength.

"Steve!" he cried. "Steve!"

But Old Glory tore free of his grip. The wind lifted it over Market Street, then hurled it against Wells Fargo's facade of glass and steel.

THE FIRST I LOVE YOU
Conrad Montell

It was the end of a long beginning for the people of Ulok, a journey from the trees of Africa to the caves above these marshlands. In four hundred thousand years, this place would be known as the Ambrona Valley of Northern Spain. For Ulok, at the dawn of that time, the valley was the "land of sweet grass and great bogs." He followed the antelope herds here. It was here that he dreamed of trapping the straight-tusked elephant. One elephant would feed twenty bands the size of Ulok's. One antelope was just enough. But Ulok had a brain that thought beyond just enough; Ulok dreamed of elephants. Only Nim, his younger son, knew words for the dream. Toog, the older son, and the others of these squat, big footed, heavy browed meat eaters called the valley "hunting place." They did not yet have words to share in dreams.

Ulok, the one of many sounds, lay dying, his wounds deep and beyond closing. As life poured out of him, the old leader passed his hunting stone to Nim, the star gazer. Toog, the strong, his heavier jaw tightening, looked at the stone as it passed to his younger brother's hand. He did not know Ulok as his father, much less any rights of a first son. Dimly, he knew he was older and of the same mother as Nim. He had not, before this, thought of being leader. But as the stone changed hands he felt a crudely formed wish for it and expressed that wish with a grunt.

There had been no meat for three days. As Ulok looked at the hungry faces surrounding him, he whispered in Nim's ear, sounds the new leader knew to mean, "Do not let them have me. Put me under the great tree." He spoke this and died.

None of the cave people had a word for dead hunter. For them, birth was a coming back, not a beginning, and death was beyond all thought. A hunter, after he died, was spoken of as "gone

101

sleeping." It was thought that he would return as fruit comes back to the tree. Till then, if times were good, he would be buried under an ancient cypress overlooking the cave.

But times were not good. It was the season of cold and there was little to hunt. Roots were difficult to dig from the frozen ground. The leopard and saber-toothed cat had famine too and grew bolder. Even the fire did not protect the cave from one saber-toothed cat that attacked at night. Ulok had driven him off but had been gravely wounded. Now he was dead and the cave people crowded hungrily around his body.

Toog pointed to the corpse. "We eat Ulok," his few words and many gestures said. The others nodded in agreement but Nim shouted, "No! Ulok must go to the great tree." Forgetting in his excitement how few of these words the others knew, he spoke of the ritual burial as Ulok had taught it to him. The cave people listened but shook their heads and they answered with gestures of hunger and moved closer to the body. In the back of the cave, one girl stopped her play with the other young ones and nodded in understanding as Nim spoke, but he did not notice her.

He stood between Ulok's body and the others. It was night. Through the fire he saw their hungry faces growing angry. They were faces he had known all his life, the only others of his kind he knew. As he watched them close in on the body, they seemed to him to be less of his kind, the kind of Ulok. They hunted together and shared meat. But there was much they didn't share. As he looked at them, he wondered how he could stop them from eating the body. He had thought that if he were lying there, Ulok would somehow stop the others and carry him to the tree.

He searched the faces for someone he could speak his thoughts to. In each pair of eyes he looked for some glint of understanding that would be for him a signal. His own mother, toothless and bent over, was in the crowd. Dimly he could remember once clinging to her. He recalled the words that had passed between them. In some not too distant cave, a mother lemur, without words, was communicating much the same to her young. Nim looked at his mother's face and knew that she was ready to eat Ulok.

He looked at Toog, his brother, and remembered their evenings by the fire learning from Ulok names for wildebeest, the giant kudu and other antelopes of the grasslands, as well as words for run, hide and other actions that made for good hunts. They learned names for the streams and mountains that bordered on the hunting grounds. Toog learned words, but he never learned the secret of how to make them grow to fit new things and for him words remained gaunt, bare bones that rarely touched his flesh. Still, as Nim looked at him, he was aware that Toog knew more words than other hunters. Toog was a plodder, different from his lighter, more agile brother and he used words the way he trod the earth, heavily and without wonder. Yet he had respect, even fear, for words as Ulok used them. When they were boys he would often hurl Nim to the ground to show his greater strength. But then Nim learned to use words as Ulok did and Toog never again put his hands on his younger brother.

Now, as he looked at Toog, Nim wondered what this strong hunter would do if he gave orders to carry Ulok to the tree. Would he have to fight Toog? He looked at Toog's massive chest and arms and considered how he might kill him in a fight. He would need a heavy blow with his stone to crush Toog's head, remembering how hard the head felt when Toog would butt him. The thought came to him that Toog might not need such a heavy blow to do the same to his head. Nim pondered this a while. It would be best, he decided, to avoid a fight with Toog.

Nim was puzzled. He did not yet have a word for "lonely," but Ulok had taught him "friend" and Nim felt a great need for this now. Toog seemed the best choice and he did not want anger between them. Toog would be angry if he did not get meat. But what of Ulok's last words? If he gave Toog the body, Nim wondered how he could face "the one of many sounds" when he returned?

Nim remembered when the saber-toothed cat had attacked the cave, other hunters had been closer than Ulok, yet they moved back. Only Ulok had jumped forward with a flaming branch from the fire to challenge the great beast. Nim thought, "Ulok has gone sleeping for the cave people. The hunters must not bring their hunger to Ulok...must do for Ulok and take him to the tree."

That his kind should do this for Ulok because of what Ulok did for them was an enormous concept for Nim. What words could he find to tell them this? "What would wise Ulok have said?"

Nim could picture the humor in Ulok's dark, deep set eyes, laughing and saying, "It is beyond me. They want meat. Can I teach them to roast words?" Yet having said this Nim knew that Ulok would somehow find the right words. He swallowed hard and spoke of Ulok's great deed as best he could. Again, there was one girl who listened and nodded with understanding. Nim saw her this time and made note of it, remembering something Ulok had said about her. The others, understanding little of what Nim said and looking hungrier than before, shook their heads and turned to Toog who was coming forward.

"We eat Ulok." There was no anger in Toog's voice only determination born of the hunger and the power of those with him. He put his gnarled hand out palm up, asking for the body, and Nim knew that Toog was not yet challenging him. It was not in Toog to challenge the order of things if this could be avoided. He and the others lacked the imagination that words had developed in Nim. They accepted the world as it was.

The sun set on one mountain, only to rise on another. Ulok had told Nim that this was not one sun at all but many, a new one each day, and on the other side of the far mountain were a pile of suns from old journeys across the sky. Nim was amazed at this wisdom but the others did not care one way or the other. It had nothing to do with meat.

Antelope were eaten yet returned to stock the herds of summer. Ulok was cold and stiff yet he would return to move again. He might return after many hunts, as a strange-looking wanderer from some far off cave. Or he might return as a new one being born and if so, why not let the women eat his heart and brain and liver to nourish and birth another? Nim remembered this lore that Ulok had passed on to him. Ulok did not want to be eaten. Still, it might not be a bad thing. Of course, he himself, hungry as he was, would not eat of Ulok. But why not let the others, especially the women, have this flesh?

This seemed a good thought and it made him feel better than if he just gave up the body for lack of power to defend it. He felt better yet in the back of his brain was the feeling that he was doing something bad. "Well," he thought finally, "I cannot fight all of them and I cannot keep Ulok's body either way. If cave people don't eat it, earth crawlers will." He moved aside and watched as Toog and another hunter lifted the body and carried it to be roasted on the fire.

The girl who seemed to understand his words watched him as he walked to the mouth of the cave. Her name was Tula. She would soon be having her first flow as a woman. The hunters had recently begun following her and she kept a distance away from them. She was aware of their eyes and suspected why they were looking at her. Tula had played at mounting with the young boys but she knew from what she saw that it would be different when the hunters came to her. What she saw of adult life she did not like much. They did not play enough; only the fire game, and after a while that grew dull to her as the same animals were called every night. While the others were looking for animal shapes in the flames or singing their one song she had noticed that Ulok and Nim went off by themselves, speaking many words and growing excited. She crept as close to them as a child dared, to listen and to learn.

She knew that when her flow started, the leader would be first to mount her. She was glad that this would now be Nim rather than old Ulok. She had become aware that Ulok had begun to notice her, and what his eyes had said frightened her and had nothing to do with his words. Still, as hungry as she now was, she could not bear to eat the body of this one whose words she had come to know. As the roasted body was being torn apart Tula retreated to the back of the cave.

It was later in the evening and the bones of Ulok had been picked clean, thirty cave people devouring ninety pounds of cooked flesh. Toog had waited for Nim, giving him respect as leader, to cut the first piece with his sharp stone. Only after seeing Nim turn his back and walk away did Toog take his own cutting stone and slice a choice piece himself. Then the others followed in order of strength and position. At the end, the weak and the old and the young, those who had neither the mind nor the heart to test their status, joined in a free-for-all for the remains.

Following the meal, each hunter selected and mounted a woman, then, after spending himself, returned to huddle by the fire with the other hunters.

Whatever desire Nim had had for a woman was lost as he

watched them gorging on Ulok's flesh. He waited at the mouth of the cave until the hunters returned from being with the women before he went to warm himself by the fire. The cave was silent now except for the snores and the belches of full bellies. Then, from deeper in the cave, he heard a high pitched song.

Everyone in the cave had his own song with sad notes or happy ones to make the few words sung seem like many. These songs were softly echoed off cave walls to lighten the sleepless part of long nights. They were sung each for oneself yet hoping to find an ear or a nod of understanding. Nim had much pain to sing about this evening but he had no stomach for his song. The voice he heard now was that of Tula and he remembered, a short time before, Ulok laughing at him and saying Nim was too much with words and the only hunter who had not seen that there was to be one more woman in the cave.

There were ten women in the cave. His mother was taboo and two others were old beyond Nim's wanting. All the rest were available as need and desire allowed. Soon there would be another. He listened to the words Tula sung. They were more than the few simple words he would have expected. They were Ulok's words, Ulok's dream of the elephant hunt, put into song. Nim wondered: could Tula understand or was she just mimicking sounds she had heard?

He got up, made a torch from a dry branch, and went to her. Tula stopped singing as he approached.

"Sing more," he said. "What song is that?"

She neither answered nor resumed singing and Nim started to go back, thinking she understood nothing he was saying. Then in the dim light he saw her eyes and knew she was frightened. He repeated his words but in a softer voice.

"It is song of Ulok," Tula said and she began singing again.

Nim listened to her and as he listened she seemed to transform before his eyes into a shape more pleasing than any he had known. Was it her singing or his desperate need that for the moment he forgot Ulok and his grief and felt as if he had just eaten of the plants that make the ground move and the eye see rainbows?

"How is it you know these words?"

"From you," she answered as she pointed to Nim, "and Ulok,"

and she pointed to the bones by the fire. Then she crouched and put a hand to her ear and with other gestures told Nim how she had often hid and listened to their words.

Nim looked at her face in the flickering light and words stopped. The cave seemed to be spinning and he felt pleasantly tired. He wanted sleep but he did not want to leave Tula, afraid that when he woke, this would be a dream and when he spoke to her again, she would be dumb. He put out his hand to touch her and see if he were sleeping now.

Tula moved back, uncertain of what he was doing. She had seen hunters hurt a woman with their hand. Though she had lived all her life in the same cave with Nim, he had never given her attention before. She moved now but then let his hand rest on her shoulder.

Nim felt her shivering and he too was cold. He went to get his antelope skins, one of which he placed around her shoulders awkwardly. Though it was a strange thing for a hunter to mount a girl before her first flow, he wanted to do this. As leader he did not have to ask, yet he found himself asking, "Is it good for Nim to stay with you?" There was fright in Tula's eyes but she nodded "yes." As he touched her she sensed his desire and then her own.

He seized her quickly in the ways he knew. Mounting and release were brief. Before this he had thought of his hunger for a woman in much the same way as his hunger for food. After satisfying himself he had always, as the others did, returned to the hunter's place by the fire. Sometimes, with Ulok, Nim had searched for words that spoke of his desire. "With a woman my heart beats as if I were chasing antelope," he once said. "Is it so with you, Ulok?" The older man had laughed and shook his head. "I cannot say," Ulok had answered, "Words are not for such things."

Nim wondered on this now as he looked at Tula. He still hungered for her after releasing his seed. They were eye to eye and Nim wondered what she was now thinking. It had never been in his thoughts of a woman to wonder this.

Tula was confused. She had always seen hunters leave quickly after releasing a woman. She had not liked it when he mounted her and was glad it was brief. There was pain and she hoped he would not hurt her again.

With a hand that was trained to harder grips, Nim ran his fingers through Tula's hair as he had seen a mother do with her young one. Tula stiffened at first. Then she opened to the pleasure of his touch. Her eyes grew heavy and closed but Nim continued stroking her hair, and then her breasts.

Across the fire, Toog was awake and he watched Nim's strange ways with this new woman, careful not to offend his brother's eyes. Then Toog met Nim's eyes and gave a respectful smile. Though a plodder, he was still willing to look at new things and learn for himself. He would wait for his time with Tula.

But his time would be long in coming. The cave people had never before formed bonds. Now, though no one yet knew it, there was to be a woman in the cave who was for only one hunter.

The cold melted into spring and the antelope herds returned to the grasslands. Game was more plentiful and it was a time when Nim, the hunter-leader, might have dreamed Ulok's dream and planned an elephant hunt. He was still new at leading the hunt and should have centered his thoughts on killing game and showing himself to be a good leader. But the brain that was bred for hunting was now cradling other offspring.

When he was not with her, Nim's mind was filled with thoughts of Tula; when he was with her, he had come to know that Ulok spoke wisely, that words were not for everything.

The other hunters had learned a new pairing of words—"Nim's woman"—and though for them there were still ten women in the cave, for Nim there was just one. He did not yet have a word for jealous but he had everything else that went with the disease. It was not enough that the other hunters had learned to stay away from Tula, even with their eyes. Her eyes were free and liked to roam. She had pleasure with Nim but now that she was a woman, she also had pleasure looking at other hunters. Besides this, Tula still wanted to play the games of her young playmates and, past a certain time with Nim, her gaze went back to them.

Nim could not bear it when the fire in her eyes shone elsewhere. Her mouth still spilled to him with words and laughter but this was not enough. When he saw her gazing at others, he would get up and join the other hunters. He could have stayed with her at those times, he always wanted to stay, but something inside him would not let him. It became painful to him to be with her and watch her look at others from the corner of her eye. This was something he had never before experienced and had no words for. He needed Tula to help him find words yet, in this, he dared not share the need with her. He was learning that pleasure is mixed with other things and there can be pain where there is no wound.

Ice was moving south and the warm seasons were short. The season of cold returned, when shadows come early and stay long. Behind shadows was the dark, the time of the saber-toothed cat, when the bravest of hunters, away from the cave fire, quickened his step and knew himself as prey. Nim had changed the way of the hunt and was away from the cave even after the sun had sunk low. It was hard to find game but there was another reason Nim's hunts took so long. It had to do with Tula. Nim noticed that the later he returned to the cave and to her, the more eager she was to see him and to be with him. Also, she was with child now and Nim sensed that her time for birth was near and he wanted to provide much meat for her to be strong. Giving birth was woman's business, he knew, but he remembered others who died when their child came.

Often, on the hunt, pictures and sounds of her seemed to come from inside him. Now, as the sun was sinking low, he thought he saw and heard her with pain and a long mouth. He wanted her to laugh with him, even beyond the tomorrow he could find words for. Many times on hunts he would wander off to find things to bring her, to make her laugh.

The other hunters did not like these ways on the hunt. Nim would take them into a canyon where there were no animal tracks, to gather little stones that the sun shone through but which were no use as tools. He would pick bright-colored plants that were too sour to eat and would carry these back to the cave. If meat was plentiful, the others would only grumble about these things. But on this hunt there had been no meat and, as the hungry unprotecting twilight deepened, they were thinking of stronger things than a grumble.

Suddenly meat was at hand; a springbok antelope was flushed

109

out of the high brush. It was a carrying female who stumbled on loose rock as the hunters chased her into a dead-end gorge. The animal looked puzzled and moved slowly, its species not yet having the instinct of fear for these meat eaters. Nim shouted commands to the others and they surrounded the now terrified animal and moved in for the kill. Sensing death, the once timid antelope lowered its horns as it charged in a desperate attempt to escape. Nim raised his stone. With skill developed in many hunts he moved swiftly, avoiding the horns while locking one arm around the springbok's throat. He started the other arm down and was an instant away from smashing the animal's skull when Nim met the springbok eye to eye and saw a face that made him stop and draw back. He saw Tula's face and seeing it made him loosen his grip and drop the weapon harmlessly. He watched the look of life pour back into the animal's eyes as it darted further up the rock between the astonished hunters. None of them had words to sound the question, "why?" but along with their hunger they knew that this was greatly wrong and they brought their anger close to Nim. Toog came forward and made a hostile sign, one which was taboo to make to the leader.

All at once Nim saw him as an enemy and raised his stone to kill Toog who was standing on the spot where the springbok had been. Toog, despite his strength, was unprepared for a life and death combat and backed off in terror, making subservient gestures to save his life. Seeing this, the rage left, and Nim dropped his arm. He trembled with feelings that were beyond his understanding. He had let a meat animal live and was about to kill his brother. His feeling were strong but now without direction. Then he turned to see the springbok slip and fall above him, wedging its hind leg as it neared the safety of the high grass. Nim bolted to it, stone again held high. The strange shapes in his head were gone and as he neared the helpless animal he saw only meat. His stone descended with a killing blow.

It was dark as they dragged the carcass back to the cave. In the distance they heard the fearsome low growl. The saber-toothed cat had smelled blood. Forgotten now were Nim's strange actions. The hunters had meat and wanted the safety of the cave. Later, their eyes would ask, "Was Nim still good to follow on the hunt?" This could not be spoken but survival required an answer.

Nim was wondering this too. Never before, except when faced with charging hyenas, had he ever surrendered meat. Seeing Tula's shape seemed as powerful as seeing charging hyenas. If he could find the words to tell her this, would she understand, would she laugh? As they entered the cave, he kept his grip on the meat. Here was something he understood fully. It was good to end a hunt with meat. With no meat, Tula would not laugh.

They finished eating the springbok and Nim began telling of the hunt. When he came to telling what he saw in the springbok's eyes, he could not find words that were true. He said, "When I looked at the springbok, I was filled with . . ." and here he wanted to say to Tula, " . . .a fear of something bad happening to you," but this was too difficult to explain so instead he said, "I was filled with a look of the leopard."

Tula understood him to be saying that he was frightened of the springbok and this was so funny to her that holding her doubly full belly, Tula laughed. Others, seeing that Nim did not grow angry, joined her. Toog did not laugh. Yet even he allowed himself to smile.

When Tula laughed, her eyes grew soft in a way that made Nim wonder if she knew more than he said. Had she perhaps really been in the animal's eye? It was, for Nim, an impossible question to ask and best forgotten. The words he spoke were not enough and yet he felt that they were too much. He was aware that words seemed to come from his mouth without his calling for them and he was aware when words were not true. When they were different from what happened, he would feel as if he had thrown good stones to the wind. Now he was sorry he had spoken. Still, it was good to tell a story and to hear Tula laugh.

He lead her from the fire to a more private space. They lay down and Nim touched her swollen belly to see if he could feel what was inside. He smiled as Tula moved his hand to a spot where he could. He stroked her in ways he had come to know would bring her pleasure. She gave him attention for a long time. Then he saw her turn to watch her playmates and, seeing this, he got up to return to the fire and the other hunters.

He huddled with them but could not keep his eyes from Tula. He wanted to go back to her but something he had yet to know as

111

pride kept him rooted. He had pain in places he had never known pain yet there was a great warm feeling mixed with the pain. His great grandchildren standing on his bones would come to name this feeling and sing of it in their songs. For Nim, it was a warm empty pain that did not go away. It lingered and his words could take him no further than to know it as a hunger for Tula.

The warm feeling gave way to cold and he moved closer to the other hunters who were already asleep and huddled next to Toog who was no longer angry with him. The other hunters would sleep the long night through but he could not find sleep. For the other hunters, huddling with one body was much like huddling with another. A young body would have more warmth but older ones, who were wiser in their need, would move together more carefully; in the end, all bodies served well. But his need now was for only one body.

The fire had been moved to the mouth of the cave to stand sentinel against the saber-toothed cat. Nim threw the fire another log. It would make the morning start easier but he did not feed the fire for that. He fed it for light, to look at Tula. She was asleep now and this bothered him. Why was she with sleep and not with him to play eye-to-eye? What had she done to give him pain and keep him from sleep? What did he want from Tula that he did not have? The words of this last question came together so clearly that Nim startled himself. He thought of waking her and mounting her but her belly had grown to where this should be taboo. Besides, it wasn't mounting her that he wanted now. He wanted just to put his hand to her breast. His cheeks grew warm as he thought of waking her for this. She might laugh in a way that would not give him pleasure. Perhaps after all, despite the taboo, he would wake and mount her. Then she wouldn't laugh in a bad way and then, before she was with sleep again he could touch her breast, play eye-to-eye and hunt for names. While he was thinking this, he heard her moan and in the dim light, he saw her put hands on her belly. Her time for the child was near and he felt there were things he must do.

He looked out the cave at the sky and his hunter eyes searched to see if he would hunt in sun or in rain when the light came. The bright stars and light wind promised a good hunt. The other hunters would be up with the first light and, with as many grunts and long looks as respect would allow, wait for him to take his eyes from Tula and begin a new hunt. Tula's moans got louder now and the thought came to him that the child would come this next hunt. As he listened to her cries he wanted to go to her and tell her he would be with her to keep the big cats and other hurtful things away. He wanted to tell her something that he could barely think himself. He could tell her that he wanted to be with her tomorrow when the sun rose over the horizon. But how could he point to the horizon beyond tomorrow and tell her he wanted to be there with her too?

Across morning embers of cave fire Nim gazed at the hunters who were casting long looks at him from the mouth of the cave. They stood together as they did every day of their lives, watching the sun rise, waiting to begin the hunt. Nim knew he had the power to make them wait, to start the hunt long after. He knew they were growing angry but they lacked the words to join their anger against him. This was good yet he felt a half-formed wish that they might some day have those words, that all the cave people could share thoughts.

From inside the cave Tula moaned and her moans grew louder. Close by were women who touched her as she moaned. Nim stood silently, midway between Tula and the hunters. He stood a long time until Toog caught his eye and grunted, pointing to the trail, then lowering his head in respect.

Nim hesitated, then walked close to him. He took his hunting stone, the stone that had once been Ulok's, and placed it in the hand of Toog. No words were spoken but all the hunters understood.

The sky and the wind beckoned the hunt. But Nim did not look at the sky or sniff the wind. He turned his back to the hunters and walked past the wide-eyed looks of the women.

As the hunters started down the trail, he was at Tula's side. He looked at her and once again felt the warmth she gave to him. But now it was not enough to feel this in silence. He needed to speak to her, not words of hunt or cave matters, or even of her child to come. He needed to speak words that told of his pleasure and then to watch her, to know if she were pleased.

"You are of good eyes Tula. You are much warm." The words

were simple yet Tula listened in wonder of their meaning. "You are for Nim," he said. "Nim is here for you."

Tula sat up, drew close to Nim and smiled. For that moment, all pain was gone. His words would be followed by others. For now, they were enough. Never in the time since words were born had the walls of a cave received ones with such a purpose. The words had been slow in leaving his lips, as if aware of their long journey to reach this place. Nim spoke them, and as he spoke, a great silence was broken.

THE YELLOW MARE
Ruth Broek

My Indian pony, May, saw the wild horses before I did. They were half way across the mountain top where trees around the spring almost hid them. Why not let May gallop over to see her old friends? She had run with them before someone caught her and sold her to the white settler whose abandoned homestead we had taken over. Sometimes I let May chase after the wild horses, but not for long, because I was afraid I couldn't stop her. I was only fifteen and had just learned to ride.

The Colville Reservation in north-central Washington had been opened to white settlement during World War I and we moved there after school was out, the spring of 1917. Dad said we were fortunate to find a place on the mountain from where he could carry out his work, which was to establish new communities and to help Indians and whites get along together. The family whose homestead we claimed had gone back to Seattle. Their mistake was to build their cabin next to an alkali lake where they became ill from the bad well water and were further discouraged because they could not make a living on land not even good for grazing cattle.

Dad had chosen a new site for our home, not in the valley but on a wide bench of land half way up against the rimrock wall of the Allotment, which was Indian tribal land. First we dug a well where Dad thought there might be an underground spring, just below a large grove of alder, birch, and ash.

We were camping this summer near that good well, out in the open within a circle of pine trees while building our house and shelters for the stock. Winters here in north-central Washington sometimes are severe, especially up on a mountain. Our camp gave a view of the valley, an ancient river course winding between stark black hills. All that was left of the vanished river was a string of lakes, of which we could see two from our home site.

Across and above Rimrock Valley was a high area of grassy valleys and lava pine ridges called the Flats. Almost every late afternoon I rode there to round up our five cows. Dad said the Flats and this Indian Allotment once must have been parts of the same mountain before that prehistoric river cut between them to gouge out Rimrock Valley. I loved to imagine the sound and sight of that river and the way it fell over the far rim which still holds our lower lake. What a tremendous waterfall it must have been!

This afternoon I had ridden to a homesteader to ask if he could work with Dad tomorrow on the new schoolhouse, which would open in the fall. Dad was there today. Otherwise we all would be helping him build something on our place, perhaps the chicken coop. Dad should have had four sons to help him pioneer this homestead instead of merely me and my younger sisters and brother of seven. Mother, of course, also helped him in everything. When he was in charge we all together made a very efficient crew, no matter what the task.

Today I felt a sense of leisure in spite of my long ride on a hot day. It was still too early to ride for the cows—only about four o'clock. I wished I knew how to get through camp without the dog barking, everyone welcoming me, delaying me, perhaps finding me some job I had to do. I wished I could go early up to the Flats because I had discovered a wonderful place, too dangerous to show my sisters and Bill. It was a hidden rock just outside one of the tall lava cores that stood like the towers of an ancient castle along the edge of the Flats. Below this bastion was a vast rock slide whch no one could climb, except rattlesnakes and chipmunks. From the base of this steep slide the land fell away and down and down through a wilderness to the Okanogan River. To be alone there was very special. I could even see the gorge into which had plummeted my no-longer-there waterfall. And sometimes an eagle hung in the sky, though it never showed me which of the black towers hid its nest.

While I was dreaming, my Indian cayuse had other ideas. Her gait had slowed into a sideways insistence that we go to the spring. All right. I gave in. May could do with a drink from the spring, and so could I. I released the reins and away she galloped, to meet her friends: I had learned not to try to guide her across this very rough mountaintop with rocks and groundhog holes. With the wild horses she had become sure-footed. One time, though, about a month ago, when I jerked May aside to avoid something, she stumbled and fell. When I came to, she was waiting, close by and worried. Just inches away, a sharp lava outcropping could have cracked my skull like an egg.

Now in August, after a rainless summer, the land was tinder dry. The bunch grass was brittle and brown between sagebrush and rocks. Scanty sunflowers made the only bright spots. A few pine were in the small valleys. Sometimes wild cherry or mock orange, not now in blossom, indicated where some moisture remained in a cleft or the shade of a rock.

It was good that Indian Jim had kept the spring open to the wild horses. It was the only place anywhere on the Allotment where they could drink. Barbed wire fences of white settlers had cut off the free range and watering holes of earlier times. Now the wild horses were waiting at the spring, watching while my buckskin pony brought me over this pathless land. To keep myself from feeling tense, I let May decide every step. Instead of watching the treacherous ground, I looked far away to the distant Sawtooth Range, which hung like a dream above the misty Cascades. Only from a high place like this mountaintop could one see them.

I hadn't been over at the spring since Big Jim and his family had gone away. Without their teepee and buckwagon, dogs, saddles, and supplies all taken away, the place seemed empty. They had left for the mountains to hunt deer and to gather nuts and fruits for the winter. Later they would move down to Nespelum where the children attended school at the Colville Indian Reservation Headquarters. In spring the family and other Indians camped down along the Okanogan River near Malott to fish and smoke their catch. Next summer our neighbors would be back here on their tribal land to gather wild roots and plants.

As we neared the spring, the wild horses waited, heads lifted, clearly inviting May to join them. I held her firmly in and she seemed to understand. Besides, after our warm ride, she was thirsty. Then, as we came close, the pinto stallion dashed off, a splendid fellow with white mane and tail. The six mares took after, beautiful creatures, their necks and legs stretched to their running. On a nearby ridge they stopped, whirled, looked back, then snorting, tossing their heads, plunged from view.

I saw that the lower end of the spring had been trampled to mud, which spread out under the trees and soon sank away within a scanty grove. The Indians had protected the spring itself by felling trees and by placing a firm log across from which to dip for their supply of water. Below this there was clear flow, which was blocked off to form a dam, almost like a trough, so wild horses and cattle could drink there without destroying the place.

Not dismounting, I let May eagerly wade out to drink of the clear water. She took her time, slurping and snuzzling, while I enjoyed the autumn shade of golden leaves above and drifting about me. A chipmunk chattered at our intrusion, then accepted our presence. A bluejay scolded, then forgot us. May switched her tail to shoo away the flies. Somewhere nearby, a warbler kept repeating a lovely song.

Suddenly May lifted her head and turned. A pale yellow mare stood not far away on a bank beyond some trees. Anxiously it whinnied. Strange! It must be one of the wild horses. I had never been so close to one before. What a beauty—a sorrel with blond mane and tail! What did she want?

Then I saw something move in the mud below her. It raised feebly, then sank away. I urged May over to see what it was. A child? An animal? Then I made out what seemed to be a very young colt, lying flat on its side, its long legs sprawled like poles, deeply sunk in the thick mud. The colt must have tried to follow its mother to the clear water but instead of taking the gradual slope it had slipped from the two-foot bank and fallen here among the trees.

Quickly I rode May out of the spring and tied her to a birch. As I came back to the bank above the colt, the yellow mare ran away, but not far. Its eyes, nostrils and mouth were full of mud. From an awful gurgling sound, I knew it must have swallowed and breathed in a lot of it.

What could I do? No one was near to help. Should I ride back to our homestead camp? But Dad was away at the schoolhouse. Mother had enough to do to care for my sisters and brother.

By now I was taking off my shoes, my riding skirt, my blouse. Why muddy my clothes? No one would see me in my under-

118

clothes. And all the while I talked to the yellow mare: "Don't be afraid of me. I'm trying to save your baby!"

But I had no tools, no shovel, nothing but my hands. I found some stout sticks and poles above the spring. I stopped to drink with cupped hands and felt the stronger for it. This time when I went back to the mud the mare did not run, but watched, as if asking me to hurry.

I looked down at the churned-up mud. It was mixed with manure, small live creatures, and goodness knows what. I hated to step into that filthy muck. Then I thought, "I must have a rope." It was an excuse, but not really. I did need a rope. I went back and untied the lariat from May's saddle. To keep my hands free, I hung the lariat around my neck. A thought distracted me as I stepped into the mud with that heavy rope around my neck: if I slipped, I too might get stuck here! The Indians might find both me and the colt in the mud next spring. And if they didn't... My laugh sounded hollow, and just then, carrying sticks and poles, I slipped, but did not fall.

I turned back then and placed the load on the bank, taking along only a digging stick. I needed to keep a free hand to grab support from a tree or overhanging branches. The uneven, slippery footing had rocks, sticks, and deep pockets hidden under the thick mud. I squashed each foot down and pulled it up with a slurpy sound.

As I began to dig out the colt's head, I forgot about myself. I tore off leaves to wipe off its ears, mouth, eyes, and nostrils—and more leaves, and more. I hardly dared look into the muddy eye; its other eye was buried deep in the mud. When I could lift the head up, I put twigs under it as a sort of matting to keep it from sinking deep again. It seemed a miracle that the poor creature was still alive. Only the gurgling sound told me that, for there was no sign of struggle. "I must hurry, hurry," I told myself as I smoothed off the mud from the soft-bristle mane of the neck.

Meanwhile, the mare called to her colt with low whinnying sounds—or was she talking to me? I took the head firmly under my arm and opened its mouth, to clean out with my fingers the tongue and teeth and throat. The colt must have swallowed and breathed in a lot of mud! Now one eye seemed to look at me; it had lashes but did not blink.

Next I dug out a leg. I had never imagined how long a baby colt's leg could be, and there were four. Each one I freed I put poles underneath so that it wouldn't sink back into the mud. All this while the colt was very quiet—fortunately. If I had had a kicking animal to work with, I couldn't have gotten it out of the mud fast enough. Each little hoof was so perfect, just the size to hold in my hand.

It took some time to dig under the body and to force sticks under it. I found that my hands worked better than sticks, so I used them, throwing the mud back, dog fashion. Every now and then I had to rest. Oh, I was tired! Then I realized that I was making progress. The mud did not flow back. It was so thick that in a few days it would be dried solid!

At last I was ready to use the lariat. I tied one end to a sturdy pole and pushed it under the colt's shoulders. But when it came through, the rope had slipped off. I tried again, this time with a forked stick, and at last the rope came through with it. Now I tied the rope around the shoulders with a non-slip knot that I had learned from a cowboy friend. At last I was ready for the big pull out of the mud.

With the other end of the lariat in my hand, and with the looped part over my arm, I climbed up onto the mud bank and went over to May. The sun was low in the sky. By now mother would be worrying about me. Perhaps she had sent the children up to the Flats for the cows, or maybe the cows had come home by them-selves, which seldom happened. Or perhaps Dad had come home early from the schoolhouse and had himself ridden up into the Flats for the cows. But just now I was too excited and too tired to care about cows.

"All right, May," I announced as I tied the free end of the lariat around the saddle horn. "Now you can do your part."

Slowly, I led her away so that the rope extended and grew taut. Then began a slow, steady pull. The colt reacted for the first time. It kicked and kicked. Hurray! Its body came loose with a swoosh and slid over the mud like a sled. Luckily I had stopped May at once so that the colt did not slam into the bank. I had forgotten that the colt would need lifting. I had to go back into the mud. I was thinking, "I can lift seven-year-old Bill, so why not this baby!" And I did, lifting it up onto the two foot bank, from the back, so that I wouldn't get kicked. The yellow mare and I were both surprised. Then, out of the mud again, I had May drag the little fellow far enough away so that it wouldn't fall over the edge again.

I had been so busy, I hadn't really looked at the colt. It looked dead! It lay there without a sign of life. In panic I tore a piece from my saddle blanket and ran over to dunk it in the spring. Back again, I swabbed out the colt's mouth, pried it open, then washed under and around the long throat, then behind the teeth. Once more I washed the cloth clean in the spring, and this time scrubbed the face and tenderly wiped the eyes. They seemed to be looking at me. Then I dug out the nostrils which still had mud in them. That did the trick. I barely had time to untie the lariat, a tough knot, when the colt kicked again. I got out of the way, fast. I stood back and watched. There seemed nothing more I could do.

I looped the lariat and tied it behind my saddle. My clean shoes I slung by their laces across my saddlehorn. My underclothes were so black with mud, I laughed as I took them off and washed them in the spring, then washed myself too. No one was watching me on all of the Allotment, and if someone was, I was so happy I didn't care. The wild mare had come to nuzzle her baby. I knew it was time to go. Perhaps I had better put on my clean blouse and riding skirt . . . .

Insistently, the yellow mare was urging her colt to get up. In her very special language, I heard her saying that a drink of warm milk would do it good. As I mounted and rode away, I looked back time and time again. I stopped every now and then, and to my joy I saw the colt actually get up, but it collapsed. The time was getting late, and I had to go. It took a while before May had reached the last rise from which I could see the spring. Then I saw—and oh, how happy I felt!—the colt was standing up on widely sprawled legs. After a while I left them there, the mare and her foal, as darkness gathered around them under a glowing, rosy sky.

WHITE AS MILK, WHITE AS COTTON

Lee Ann Johnson

It was in August, while sunning in the backyard, that Lynn saw the first snake. The gliding motion registered in the corner of her eye; the hairs prickled on the back of her neck. Turning her head very slowly, she saw the snake about ten feet away.

A chill swept across her back and arms, and she froze on the chaise. She knew it was a water moccasin, felt it in the pit of her stomach even before her eyes fixed on its dull olive banding. The snake's head was repulsive, shaped like a wedge: very flat, very black.

Careful, she told herself. Don't alarm it. Just swing your legs down slowly, then run for the house. The magazine across her legs slid onto the edge of the metal frame with a soft thud. The snake stiffened, rearing back its head. Its mouth unhinged, and all she could see was white, a cavernous milky mass of throat and teeth and fangs. The tail began to beat with rhythmical precision.

Lynn screamed and bolted. She locked the porch door behind her and ran to the kitchen phone. Rob tried to calm her, said to stay inside; he'd come home early.

She shivered even when he held her. Together they looked out the glass porch at the yard sloping gently toward the woods. Nothing. They went upstairs to their bedroom windows and stared down. Rob blinked. He pointed to three splotches in the yard, coiled like darkened garden hoses. Lynn saw them, too.

From the closet he withdrew the shotgun and loaded it while she sat on the bed remembering the snake's vicious glare and the dry, shiny white of its mouth. She didn't go to the window when Rob went downstairs, even after she heard the shots.

"I got them all; they were damned big, three and four feet. I shoveled them into the garbage can." Rob's voice was as thin and taut as steel wire when he came up. He went into the bathroom

122

and washed his hands for a long, long time.

When he came out, he sat beside her on the bed, barely touching.

"I can't stand them, they're so scary," she said, squirming. Her dark eyes were wide with fear.

"They're dead now. Don't worry."

"We should have stayed in the apartment."

"Come on, you wanted a house as much as I did."

"But not this one! I told you there'd be snakes in the woods. And these are poisonous!"

"Lynn, there's nothing to be so upset about. Everything's going to be all right. They're gone," he tried to soothe her. "They're gone." But he kept glancing at his hands.

After a while Rob phoned the neighbors. The Steiners weren't home, but he spoke to the unfriendly widow on the right.

"She sees a couple of cottonmouths in her yard maybe once a year. She guesses they go back to the pond in the woods. She doesn't know anything about disposing of them." He pressed his lips together. "I want you to be careful. They're probably coming out because it's so hot."

The next morning Lynn awoke early and crept to the window. There was a dark gash midway up the yard. She stared hard, saw that it was moving.

"Rob!" she cried out, turning to the bed. "Rob, there's another one!"

"Shit!" He came to her side groggily. "Keep your eye on it while I get the gun." When he returned from the backyard, Lynn set the kitchen table but neither could eat.

"Why don't you go to Val's and study?" he said, trying to sound offhand but not succeeding. "You could sit out by the apartment pool."

She nodded, knowing her college friend would be home, and said she might. He kissed her, told her he would call at lunchtime. Then he went out to the garage. As he bent to pull the door up he saw something move. He sprang back in time to see a snake glide under the raised foundation.

His knees felt like rubber as he ran to the front door and pushed it open. "Lynn," he shouted. "I'm taking you to Val's. Now!"

From Val's he called an exterminator. "Look," Rob explained

as calmly as he could. "There are cottonmouths—water moccasins —coming up into my yard. There's one under the house. Can you spray for them?"

"Nothin' we can do but shoot 'em, mister. Thirty dollars a housecall, twenty-two fifty per hour after the first thirty minutes. You want someone out?"

"What I *want* is something to keep them away for good. A chemical, some poison. Isn't there anything like that?"

"If there is," the man pondered, "we ain't got it." Then his voice cheered. " 'Course we haul the bodies away. It's up to you."

Rob dialed the Steiners, his neighbors next door. He meant to warn them and hoped for advice. When he hung up the phone, Lynn knew something was wrong.

"He was surprised we didn't know," Rob said, a strange look on his face. "According to him the snakes have been coming as long as he can remember. Every August. He takes a hoe to them."

"Every August!" cried Lynn.

"Ugh!" Val exclaimed. "How could he *do* that?"

"He kills two or three 'waifs' a summer. That's what he calls them."

"They're hardly waifs," Lynn protested. "More like legions. We've had five already!"

"That's just it." Rob worked his mouth as though trying to rid a bitter taste. "That's why he thought we knew. He said each time the snakes come back, it's our house they head for!"

"No!" Lynn cried. A chill spread at the base of her spine.

"Lynn," Rob began, but his voice went nowhere.

"Now wait," Val said. "What exactly do the snakes *do*?"

"Gather under the foundations, where it's cool. He said they nest there."

"Do they lay eggs?"

"Not that he knows of. They just rest. And molt."

"How *long*, Rob?" Lynn's voice came as from the bottom of a well.

Rob sagged. "A week to ten days, maybe. Then they're gone. Look, Lynn," his words came in a rush, "the sellers concealed all this—."

"I don't give a damn about the sellers, we've got to get out! Don't you realize what you're saying? Your great bargain," she hesitated, then flung it at him. "It's a snakepit, Rob. We bought a snakepit!"

At the law firm where he was a second-year associate, Rob requested more time on the documents he was drafting. Then he asked his secretary to hold all calls while he telephoned the state university. He was connected with a professor in the herpetology department who listened attentively.

"Snakes do react to natural disturbances, Mr. Wagner—land movement, excessive heat or rainfall, that sort of thing. But I've never heard of moccasins in Florida gathering year after year."

"Well, I've got them now. Is there anything I can do to keep them away? A fence? Cement the foundation?"

"Not if the ground's soft, as you say; they'd burrow under. I'd make sure all the foundation vents are closed; they can wriggle through pretty easily."

The lifeless bodies rose before Rob, balanced on his shovel. They began to slither out of the garbage, across the smooth cement floor of the garage. Rob closed his eyes and massaged the bridge of his nose. Then he drew a breath and asked what bothered him the most.

"Professor, could the moccasins be laying eggs on my property?"

The professor chuckled. "If they are, it's a first. Moccasins bear live. And they don't move around then."

"But I don't mean to mislead you, Mr. Wagner." The voice came over the wire, apologetic. "Snakes *do* migrate, at least in very cold climates. They'll 'den' together in an old cellarhold, for example, and return to it each year."

"Oh?" Rob inhaled.

"They'll come from miles around, thousands of them. And hibernate for months, until the ground has thawed. So you see," the professor said, "you're lucky to be where it's warm."

Once the sourness had left his mouth, Rob closeted himself in the firm library, consulting the major authorities on real estate law. Then he sought out the senior partner in litigation.

"The problem is, Florida's not a liberal jurisdiction," the partner said, shaking his head. He leaned forward, his elbows planted in the soft glow of his polished desk. "You're a lawyer;

you've studied 'caveat emptor.' "

"But the sellers had a duty to disclose. The fact that snakes descend on the house year after year is as material and as damaging as if it were built on swampland."

The partner tilted back in his chair, his chin delicately balanced on the tips of his fingers. "You say it was priced twenty thousand under market but you didn't ask why. And you've been in it five months. I don't think, even were you to prevail on the law, that the court could rescind the sale. The defense will argue that the house is habitable fifty weeks a year. My guess is defendants would be liable only for out-of-pocket expenses."

"Expenses!" Rob exclaimed. "I want the bastards to pay for everything!"

"Against any potential recovery, Rob, you'll have to weigh the time and money spent in litigation. And the emotional energy. It'll be particularly draining to hear the defense remind the jury at every turn that you're a lawyer, that you should have been more cautious."

The partner stopped, seeing Rob's face. He rose and patted him on the arm. "I'm sorry if I sound cold, but you wanted a quick opinion. You'll need to do some hard thinking about whether to pursue the matter. I'll give it some thought, too."

Stomach churning, Rob took the rest of the day off. On the street just before Val's he narrowly missed a bicyclist. When Lynn saw his hunched shoulders she prescribed a bottle of wine, which the three of them drank in the shade of the patio. Rob ran his fingers through his hair as he told them what he'd learned.

"So crime pays," Val said dryly. "My advice to you two, then, is to burn the place down, collect the insurance, and walk away!"

"Swell. Except I was informed today not to forget, because a jury won't, that I'm a lawyer."

Lynn's voice cut in like a knife. "Can the snakes get *inside* the house? Crawl up stairs?"

"I'll make sure they can't."

"Rob, it's not worth it! I'm not going back there."

"I told her you're both welcome to stay here as long as you like," Val said.

Rob turned from one to the other. "Okay," he said wearily. "Thanks."

He looked directly at Lynn. "We *are* going home. Eventually. Meanwhile I want to drive over. If the snakes are burrowing *under* the house, I ought to be able to get in and pack a bag."

"Rob, don't!"

"It's okay, I'll call the exterminator for protection. I'm not—." He stopped and swore sharply, her unspoken accusation hammering in his head. "I'm not going to do anything more foolish."

They broke camp at Val's two weeks later, after paying a cleaning service to scour the grounds of their house and inspect inside. In the first hours they treaded nervously through the rooms, Lynn insisting that they check everything. Rob kept the shotgun by his side as he opened each closet door, each cupboard, each dresser drawer. Lynn stood back warily, unable to relax. She saw snakes everywhere, curled like coathangers, taut like broomhandles, but they were only in her mind.

That night Rob pulled back the bedcovers and entered first, carefully smoothing a place for her. Only after he searched the bed a second time would she lie down, her body rigid.

"They were in this room," she whispered. "I know it."

"Shh, they were outside. Don't think about them."

Lynn stared at the ceiling. "I can't help it. The thought of our lying here, trying to curl up, gives me goosebumps. It's just like the snakes."

"Turn your mind off and try to sleep. Tomorrow'll be a lot easier."

"Rob?"

"Hmm?"

"Have you thought what this means? That we can't ever have a baby here?"

"Shh, don't worry about that now. A family comes after you graduate, you know that. We've got time to work it out."

She sighed heavily, still staring at the ceiling.

"I'm afraid, Rob," she whispered, and he felt her tremble. He pulled her to him and held her tightly, a long long time, until she was safely asleep.

Early the next morning, while Lynn was still in bed, Rob examined outside. Dressed in robe and sneakers, carrying the shotgun, he moved slowly along each side of the house. The

August sunshine was bright enough for him to see several feet under the foundation, and he used a flashlight to illuminate the rest. He felt foolish, skulking around his own home.

It surprised him that his heart was pounding so, particularly since he saw nothing as he inched along. He didn't know what traces the snakes had left, hadn't wanted to ask, but whatever there had been the cleaning service had removed.

In the backyard he walked more swiftly, confident that the snakes had withdrawn. He marveled that their advance and retreat from the house should be as predictable, as orderly, as his and Lynn's own. The snakes' claim to the house was superior, prior in time to theirs. We're all seeking a nesting ground, he thought; it's the elemental urge to nest. He turned back from the soft edge of the lawn, towards the house, and something moved under his sneaker.

The hair on his neck rose in hackles. He looked down to see the tip of a narrow greenish tail slither past and burrow into the woods. He closed his eyes and shuddered. A baby! was all his mind could think before he willed his legs back up the lawn in great detached strides. For the first time he felt the staggering force of the snakes, saw them propagating and returning relentlessly, this year forty, next year a hundred, tangled and coiled, coiled and recoiled, undermining his very being.

At the porch door he paused disheveled, his breath coming in spurts. There was only one thing to do: kill them one by one, kill them until there wasn't a single snake left that could remember and show others the way. He turned, glaring at the woods. The house was his, goddamit; he wouldn't run again.

In the fall, when they no longer lived on tiptoe, Rob told Lynn over and over that his plan would work. He would find someone to help him kill the snakes. They had saved so long for a home, she had worked so hard to put him through school: the house was their new beginning. Besides, he admitted, putting it on the market would mean taking a beating, if they could unload it at all. Even filing a lawsuit would be too expensive and too uncertain.

"Then we should put up a sign and move out," Lynn argued. "Not tell anything."

"We can't. You know that."

"Maybe you couldn't, but I could! I wouldn't have thought so before, but I could! And I could walk away from the house, too, let the bank have everything. It wouldn't be the worst thing that ever happened. At least then my nightmares would stop. At least we could be ourselves again!"

"I'm not going to let the snakes drive us out!"

"Drive us out? Rob, look what they've done to us. We're growing scales even as we stand here!"

He groaned. "Lynn, we've got to stay. I'm asking you to stay."

"You mean 'stay' as in 'stuck.'"

"No, goddamit, I don't! I mean we'll beat the snakes at their own game, assuming they even come back. After that it won't be long until you finish school and I find out my partnership chances. *Then* we can move if we want, and we won't lose our shirts if we do. Trust me!"

"And what happens in August? You chop up snakes below, and I dream horrors upstairs? I couldn't bear it. I *won't* stay here then, and I don't want you to, either."

"Well, you could go somewhere nearby for a couple of weeks. Call it a vacation."

She hesitated, and there was pain in her face and voice when she spoke. "I'll stay for now, but when it's time you must go with me. It'll cost money, I know, but for God's sake, go with me. Let someone else do the killing!" Her eyes swam, and when at last she saw him nod, she felt she had been fighting for her life.

The following August they began an uneasy countdown, trying to guess when the snakes would come. Finally they closed the house and drove down the west coast of Florida earlier than planned, to ease the tension. Lynn spent hours each day on the beach, lulling her senses with the plash of the waves. She lost herself in reading.

When they turned into their driveway, everything looked immaculate. The lawn was freshly mowed; the windows sparkled in the sunlight. They moved cautiously through the house, but Lynn tried to tell herself it was only a formality: the exterminators reported the snakes gone. Rob opened and looked into all the drawers, all the closets, and he laughed. They were acting like sneak thieves.

The next day, after Rob went to work, Lynn spent the morning running errands, saw Val in the afternoon. In the evening, when Rob called to say he would be late, she busied herself with the laundry. It was good to be back, she told herself; she mustn't think about why they had gone.

She played the stereo loudly, so that she could hear it up in the bedroom where she sorted and folded the clean clothes, making neat mounds which she tucked carefully into dresser drawers. She pressed Rob's shortsleeved shirts, thinking of the beach where they had been. She ironed the colorful sundress she had worn when they picnicked on the seawall.

Afterward she drew a bath and sank into the soft, perfumed bubbles, her tanned body growing supple in the warmth. She thought of the hectic semester about to begin, of classes back to back and lunch on the run. There would be so little time.

She rose and stepped from the bath, reaching for a towel from under the counter. As she wrapped herself in its folds, something grazed against her arm. Her flesh crawled and she dropped the towel. Something rustled to the floor. It was white as milk, white as cotton, a slender molted skin as papery as ash.

"Oh!" Lynn cried out, looking down. Her eyes rolled back. "Oh!" she screamed again. And again.

When Rob came home, she did not know his name.

THE MAYOR'S LIMOUSINE
Dexter H. Mast

I had been a Desk Sergeant for over two years in the Oakland, California Police Department and could now take the next Lieutenant's examination. I would have had a good chance of passing except that in a burst of Boy Scout honor I had refused to fix a traffic ticket for the Mayor that one of my men, Mervin, had given to a friend of the Mayor. The Mayor as an attorney had taken the case to court. I had discovered a witness who testified, and the judge found the Mayor's friend guilty on all counts. Mervin told me, "I shuddered as the judge slowly read and pronounced sentence on each count. He really got it."

Now the Mayor had just called asking me to assign a police officer to drive him and his wife to the Senator's party in the Mayor's Limousine stored in the police garage. The year was 1954. Big city mayors were driven to civic functions in limousines by uniformed police officers.

When the Mayor called, I had promptly answered the phone: "Sergeant Mast, Oakland Police Department speaking."

"John speaking, Dexter. I want to use the limousine tonight. My wife and I have been invited to the Senator's home for a party. Get me a chauffeur and have him at my place at 7:15. Oh, and before the officer picks us up, have him stop at the Go-Go Cleaners and pick up my wife's gown. Can you do that for me, Dexter?"

I was relieved to hear the friendly tone of his voice—maybe all was forgiven. Then I looked at the situation board on the wall opposite my desk. I did not have anyone to assign as a chauffeur.

"No I can't, John, because there are no officers available. What happened to the traffic man assigned to that duty?"

The Mayor said, "I don't have an assigned driver now." (I learned later that there had been a disagreement between the assigned driver and the Mayor. He wanted the officer to clean the limousine while waiting for the Mayor.)

I suggested, "Why don't you use your personal car and drive yourself and wife to the party?"

Over the phone I could feel his honor, the Mayor, doing a slow burn.

Well under control, the Mayor asked, "Are there any command officers on duty, a Chief? a Captain? a Lieutenant?"

The day was Sunday and all the Chiefs, Captains and Lieutenants had taken off, except for old "Sugar Lips" who was watch commander. He had left me in charge about an hour before the Mayor called, informing me that he was leaving headquarters on police business and would be gone for several hours.

"No, John, there are no command officers on duty. I'm in charge."

Then I thought: This is the Mayor and one of the emoluments of his office is a limousine driven by a police officer. Besides, my chances of advancing in rank seemed a little dim. So I told him, "I will do my best and get you the first available man."

The Mayor repeated his instructions: "I want the limousine in front of my door at 7:15 with my wife's gown. You understand that it is very important that I be at the party!"

When the Lieutenant left on his police business, the situation board had shown most of the patrol cars blue—available. I was not alone at headquarters. I had Jerry, the civilian watch clerk, a tall, kindly, middle-aged man who handled the paper work for the third watch. The Lieutenant had also left me with two citizens waiting to see him on important police matters.

I called the first citizen to my desk. He was a young man with a baby face and effeminate manners, who broke down and cried as he said, "I want police protection while I remove my things from a room that I share with another fellow." I called in an officer to go with him and keep the peace, telling him, "See that this queen does not get hurt. We've had four homicides already in the last six months, and we can't afford another one."

After the first citizen was taken care of, a middle-aged woman approached my desk. She was well-dressed, proper in manner, medium height and build, gray-haired and very sincere. She had a complaint against her neighbors. "They are communists," she told me in a confidential whisper. "They are experimenting with a death-ray machine. I know this because when they turn on their machine, I can feel waves of heat go over me."

I told her she should write it all out on paper, so that the police would have a record to work with. Jerry took over the lady, giving her a pencil and pad of paper, putting her in a comfortable school chair and getting her started with a proper heading.

About six p.m. the police radio gave out a 940B, officer needs help, urgent! Headquarters monitored all police radio calls. The 940B could mean anything from a shootout to citizen refusing to be arrested. The 940B was an excuse for the younger officers to turn on their red lights and sirens, then go full speed ahead down the middle of the street TO THE RESCUE. Too often it meant that a car or cars would pile up and someone would be hurt. This time the trouble was a small riot in the West End over a traffic ticket, and two police cars, responding to the call, ran into each other. This took two cars and four men out of service for at least two hours, with paper work. The district sergeant was also involved.

Slowly, one at a time, the blue lights blinked out on the situation board and red lights took their places. I looked over toward traffic division which was on the same floor as patrol division. No one was there. Everyone had gone home. Jerry and I and the lady who was writing were the only ones left to keep the flag flying at headquarters; and with the board all red, the Mayor wanted me to get him a police officer to drive him and his wife in the Limousine to the Senator's party.

The first man hit back in service at 6:40. I called the radio room sergeant to have that man come in and get the limousine to the Mayor as soon as possible. The radio room sergeant objected. I told him that I'd explained our situation to the Mayor, and that the Mayor had insisted. I also reminded the sergeant that the decision was my responsibility.

Time was passing. The Mayor lived in the suburbs, and I doubted that the limousine would get to his house before 7:30; and if the driver had to get gas, which he did—a small disaster.

Headquarters radio monitor informed me that the Mayor's chauffeur had hit off duty, on my orders, at the police garage at 6:50. Our one blue light went red, then out.

Minutes later the radio room sergeant called me. "What are you going to do now, sergeant? We have a 906 (person breaking in), a hysterical woman is on the line. I'm going to tie you into this line and increase the volume for the tape. The complainant has barricaded herself in her room. She lives on the beat of the man you took off duty to drive the Mayor's limousine, Sergeant!"

I again looked at the situation board. It was all red. The thin line of police protection had vanished. The man on the mike was repeating over and over: "Any car, any car, a 906 code 3 at 331—Seventh Street, Apartment 20."

I heard over my phone the woman sobbing—the phone being dropped. Then over her sobs I could hear the splintering of wood. The crash of a body against a door. The door was shattering. A man cursed the woman, calling her by name; then a shriek, cries, pleading. The thumping of a mad drummer on a muted drum. Then quiet, except for a gurgling sound in a diminishing cadence, which in time gave way to silence.

A car came on the air, then another, to take the 906 call, which we now knew was 187—Murder.

Someone was trying to get my attention. The writing lady was asking if she could come back the next day to finish her report. She had a lot more to tell. I nodded my head. She went out, very happy. It was seven o'clock. Jerry, who had been listening on his phone, was crying.

The writing lady had been gone a half-hour when the lieutenant came in, carrying himself like an officer and a gentleman, smelling of perfume. As he passed my desk he asked if there was anything doing.

"Not now," I said, and the lieutenant went into his office.

The next day, Monday, my captain, Howard, called me at my home and said, "I am writing a letter of reprimand to the chief for your actions last night."

The written reprimand would be placed in my personal folder, which meant that I could not take the next lieutenant's examination.

Strange: Captain Howard's announcement did not seem unfair. The captain was essentially a fair man whom I admired.

"The Mayor told me that you were rude and uncooperative, that you failed to instruct the chauffeur to pick up his wife's gown at the cleaners as requested. They had to pick up the gown and go to his office at the City Hall where she changed. The strain of all this, caused by your inefficiency, made the Mayor's wife ill, and she became hysterical at the Senator's party."

Someone else was using my voice to ask the Captain: "DID SHE DIE?"

THE ARTIST
Richard Gold

I keep bumping my head—on iron lamp posts, brick buildings, hard stuff. I seem to have lost control. I float between a quarter-inch and ten feet above the ground, just another particle in the yellow air swirling over the city, a six foot long particle, thirty years old. It's distressing. It's distressing, but each crack of my skull against steel, iron, or brick increases my determination to respond. A battered floater is not without gentle contacts, some-times settling onto mown grass or the lap of a friend. There are moments when things can be done, or remembered—though explanations of my condition remain elusive. I wear a green T-shirt with a hole above the navel, blue jeans, leather boots.

Once I clutched the second floor ledge of a doctor's office on Piedmont Avenue. Black grit stained my palm. My body rippled like a flag. The doctor came to the window, smiled, and walked away. I feel sure he went to consult his medical journals, confi-dent of finding the answer. I did the backstroke, on my way across town, to west Oakland, the ghetto, where the kids threw rocks.

Someone suggested I do photography, aerial pieces, of west Oakland for example—the ship propellors stacked outside the foundry as gears that make brown children run across vacant lots—neon-lit bars in a row of unpainted buildings, staggering stairways to second floor flats, ripped shades, wash on the lines. But I'm prejudiced against aerial shots, they explain nothing. I want to get little, to capture the tiniest reflection on a polished propellor, to isolate the sine wave of a sagging house. Let that be my art piece, something small.

The fight. Is the fight an explanation, is that moment why I'm here, here, and here: west Oakland, Lake Merritt, the M&B Shopping Center? If so, how did I get there, the Arena, into the

135

ring, wearing baggy red trunks, blue waistband, overmatched against a black man with cement muscles, one tough guy. I was pinned in a corner. The uncovered ropes scraped my back, tiny fibers piercing my skin, while my opponent danced at the end of his reach. His strength flowed in a rhythm, focused at the moment his fist touched my temple, again, again, and again—while my own energy flowed, a cool shiver, a single wave traversing my body—until one punch, the punch that took a year to arrive, focused my energy into the exhalation that fluttered my extended lips, became a butterfly, escaped.

I sought escape in the Montclair Hills, where houses lined the rims of overgrown ravines. There breezes carried me along winding roads, above toy-like sports cars in bright colors. I floated closer to the houses and, though they were alike, built by one contractor, I saw them as sanctuaries, temples of the private life. I was reassured. My own existence, wanderings and concussions could not be shared; perhaps the domestic promise of Montclair would compensate for this fate, inside a house with closed windows, preferably air-conditioned.

I descended then, toward the asphalt drive and slate walk, a square lawn and juniper, and under the impetus of a playful breeze, I followed a woman through an open door. She carried two bags of groceries, reeling across a shag rug to the kitchen. The woman wore a brown knit outfit, matching heels. Her hair was styled in an unnatural shape. I noticed a precision in her appearance that mirrored the order of her kitchen: gleaming appliances, paper products, plastic decorations, padded floor. I despaired. Then the woman turned and saw me. She said, "Oh, oh, oh." She ran, and I floated after. Convection currents? Coincidence? I floated after her, from room to room, past unused furniture and self-help books—until in the bathroom she fell, sprawled across the rug-covered toilet seat, surrounded by brilliant porcelain. She reached for the bowl brush, its white plastic handle decorated with a *fleur-de-lis*. "Stop," I said. She stiffened, she smiled. "Stop." I bumped my head on her smile. She dropped the brush. "Stop."

For an art project I took a section of clear plastic shower curtain, textured with tiny bumps, and applied heat to make it blossom, the beginnings of a bubble, to represent my sun-burnt and wind-burnt skin over San Francisco Bay, painted in three flesh tones. I could touch the plastic with a finger, and it would respond, sensitively. I painted "WELCOME" in black to finish the piece.

Did the drugs create a moment that explains why I'm here, here, and here: the estuary, Rockridge, the Buttercup Bakery? How could the drugs be an explanation when their effect was so elusive? Were they ever even a part of my life? What first brought me into the basement apartment—cold cement painted red, mattress on the floor, army sleeping bag? I sat on a swivel chair, by an oak desk overflowing with pills and powders. On the floor were clear plastic pillows, ten pounds each of marijuana.

Filling a bone pipe with red Colombian, I watched it glow redder beneath a match. I inhaled, felt shoved to the bottom of a muddy crater, with no one to talk to. This was good, and I wanted to go further. Speed is the pursuit of an ever-receding There; from my desk drawer I removed a bottle of white crosses. These opened my eyes with their grab at my stomach. My body questioned my intentions. I ignored the rebellion. A rhythm was establishing itself now, my brain hummed, and I drew to me a white mound of cocaine on its marble platter. Reaching for a razorblade, I chopped the powder fine, shifting it back and forth across the marble into two equal lines. This drug numbed my nose, the back of my throat, my palate. It produced a cool shiver, removed my shoes. It promised power.

I sought power downtown, floating among structures of reinforced glass, concrete, and steel, where everything reached upward like the waves grasping for my body over San Francisco Bay. Could I ally myself with this solidity, make peace with obstructions and sharp edges? Pushed along by noon crowds, I searched among the people for a snide scuff on a heel, an errant thread on a shoulder, a telltale stain on a tie, and I found none. I maneuvered into a lobby, floated up a stairwell, did a frantic dog paddle through an open door.

The man behind the desk had his back to me. I heard his discrete mastication, saw the pulsing muscles in his neck. "Lunch?" I asked. The man twisted around, his left hand covering his mouth and the bottom of his nose. On that hand was painted a smile. His right hand was extended in manly greeting. He turned away. Again I heard him working his dry mouth, and again I asked, "Lunch?" Again he faced me, hidden behind the painted smile. I performed a shy back-flip. He turned away.

The art piece matured into an assortment of black and brown portfolios, leather and plastic, open and empty, hungry, mounted in a Samsonite frame. I painted "WELCOME" in white to finish the piece.

Is the BART train an explanation, an escape, a rejection, a part of my life? Does it explain why I'm here, here and here: the Short Stop on Fruitvale, the Quick Stop on 14th Avenue, the Stop and Go on Foothill Boulevard? Did I jump or was I pushed in front of that commuter-carrying silver snake? The collision sent me tumbling in the air above the tracks, only to fall again before the on-rushing train. For this second collision, and those that followed, I braced myself with knees drawn, pushed off against the engine with my feet, and leaped gracefully ahead.

Collision after collision, the diving motion became so repetitive I performed it unconsciously, moving with the suburbanites back and forth under the bay. Never worried about the destruction of my body, I was threatened rather by the tedium: what incentive had I for getting small, for understanding iron tracks on a uniform gravel bed? The noise was constant. The people on the platforms were always the same. The lights underground burned my eyes.

For an art piece I painted the BART tunnel with photoemulsion, over the lights that burned my eyes, and exposed a series of images along the walls. Thus, I created a motion picture for moving people. It had a special topic, treated in a special way: the period of my catatonia.

That time began with a "pop." Was I going to a college class or to the dentist? Bicycles, sidewalk walkers, and busses all snapped into slow motion; birds too. I was still completing my footfall when some men laid me in an ambulance and took me away. Of the centuries in the institution, little can be said: I saw the flight of a scoop of mashed potatoes onto a plate, the growth of a saliva bubble between a pinhead's lips, a nurse's fingernail forever moving between her front teeth.

There was one hope and dread during that period. I knew where the institution's guard kept a gun in a desk drawer. I knew where the nurse hid the key to that desk. I knew that with seventeen years' concentrated effort I would be able to move from hiding place to desk, to hold a gun in my hand, point it against my temple. Could I do it? Killing myself would have been easy, but I wondered: could I listen to the month long report that would rock my inner ear? Could I endure for another month the crack of shattered skull? For how many years would I experience the projectile travelling through the soft tissue of my brain?

That was my movie, thoughtful immobility to affect the weary transient. That was my movie, but that was not my art, nothing so conventional: I created a performance piece, with the movie as background. For additional props I went to the foundry, cast a hand-held catapult and dozens of bronze gherkins. I was particularly proud of the patina on the pickles.

The day of the performance arrived. I was leaping and diving along the BART tracks. Just before plunging into the tunnel, I pulled out the catapult and began shooting pickles at the train, shot pickles at the people on the Oakland West platform. The pickles flew. "Death," I cried. "Death!" People screamed. People laughed or were puzzled. All were repulsed when the warty *objets d'art* landed vibrating at their feet; I disappeared, travelling under San Francisco Bay, to accomplish the finale of my piece. There, in the tunnel that was now my movie, I shot the most lovely bronze gherkins of all, one after another, carefully aimed, at the sequentially stationary image of my palpitating heart. I called the piece "The Conquest of Time."

NOTHIN' BUT A BOB
Gwen Jordan

11:45 PM January 15

DDDRRING! DDDRRING!

"Police Emergency. May I help you?" came the impersonal response.

The man's voice was loud and agitated. "Please send the police to 1221 Linden Lane. I just shot a prowler."

The automatic recording device sounded its first BEEP!

"What is your name, please?" the dispatcher asked.

"Nate Walker. There's a man out...."

BEEP!

"Your address?" asked the dispatcher.

"I've already told you. Are you going to send someone over?"

BEEP!

"Repeat that address, please."

BEEP!

"1221 Linden Lane. Will you hurry?"

BEEP!

"Please remain on the line. A unit is being sent to your location right now. When they arrive and announce who they are, please have the officer speak to me," she said.

"Right! Just please hurry. That guy could bleed to death."

11:51 PM

The paramedics hoisted the semiconscious form onto the gurney, then into the ambulance. The young boy's dark features were contorted in agony.

"Am I gonna die?" he managed to ask through his grimace.

"Hang in there, fella. You're gonna be alright," the attendant at his head said with a faint smile. "We ain't lost nobody yet, tonight."

11:52 PM

Officer Daniels placed the receiver on the telephone. He shifted his gun belt more comfortably on his hip before speaking. His roving eye spotted the .22 pistol on the coffee table in the living room. He nodded to his partner who retrieved the weapon. Turning to Nate, he asked, "Is that the gun?"

Nate nodded.

"Mr. Walker, can you tell me what happened?"

"Well, this guy and two more were fooling with Dad's van," the young man began. He dabbed at the perspiration that beaded on his forehead and ran down the side of his face. His once white handkerchief was now yellow and dank.

"Is that the one in the driveway?"

"Yeah, that's it. They were trying to steal the tires off of it."

"Okay, fine. Just tell me what you did about it."

Nate licked his lips. His nostrils twitched nervously. It had happened so fast.

He remembered the scurrying, muffled sounds stealing through the chill of the midwinter night. Crouching in the shadows of the living room, he snuck a peek through the curtains at the picture window. His parents were away for the weekend. They had been so upset when the van was firebombed the night before. Why would anyone do such a thing? Joseph and Clara Walker were good people who minded their own business. Nate shook his head in the gloom as he strained to listen, wondering what caused the faint sounds. The crunch of a footstep on the gravel of the driveway assured him that his ears were not deceiving him. Someone was out there near the van. He peeked out again. He saw first one form, then two others moving stealthily in the darkness. He eased over to the door, gently opened it a crack, and was momentarily blinded by the splash of moonlight that coursed its way into the darkened room.

"C'mon, man," said the frantic, yet low-pitched voice from the front of the van. "Get that thing over here so we can get outta here."

"Quiet, man. You makin' enough noise to wake the whole damn neighborhood." This time the voice hissed from a shadowy form near the passenger side of the disabled vehicle.

Nate flung open the door and assumed a firing postion. Simultaneously he yelled, "Stop, you bastards!"

"What the fuck?" one of the voices managed, then all three began running. One of the boys stumbled in his haste and lost his balance.

"Stop, I say, or I'll shoot!" Nate called.

The boys continued their flight. The one who had stumbled at the foot of the driveway was just regaining his feet when the explosion hit him above the left kidney. His stride collapsed and he tumbled into a heap just beyond the lip of the driveway.

7:10 PM January 16

Claudine Jeffers looked down at the sleeping form of her mangled son. She was thankful he was alive. The doctor had promised he would walk, but little else. He had lost that left kidney and much much more. The bullet had ricochetted about his abdominal cavity, causing irreparable damage. Claudine tightened her lip and shook away the tear that threatened a deluge if she lost control.

The nurse who monitored the condition of the two patients in this room in ICU silently went about her duties. She readjusted the tube implanted in her patient's abdomen.

Claudine felt sick to her stomach as she watched the dark fluid pouring from her son into the machine at the foot of his bed. The nurse looked up at her and attempted a half-hearted smile.

"Don't worry, Ma'am. He's resting just fine."

Claudine's eyes brimmed but did not spill. She turned and rushed from the room.

9:25 AM

Inspector Daniels finished Mirandizing Nate. "Having these facts in mind, will you talk with me about this offense?"

"Yes, sir," came the soft reply. The young black man appeared composed and in control. For what seemed the twentieth time, Nate recounted the events of the past two nights, beginning with the firebombing and ending with the shooting of Albert Jeffers.

"Now, son," the Inspector began, "why did you shoot?"

"They were trying to steal the tires off the van."

"How did you know that?"

"They had a bumper jack under it. Didn't you guys find it

when you were at the house?"

"Oh, yeah. We found it." Daniels was quiet for a moment, his brow furrowed. "Do you think that was a good enough reason to shoot someone?"

"Seems to me that's the chance you take when you get caught wrong like they were. They had no right to steal something that wasn't theirs."

Inspector Daniels sucked hard on the toothpick his tongue turned at the corner of his mouth. "You think those boys were the ones who bombed your folks' van?"

"You got any better suspects, man?"

Daniels spat out the shredded slivers of the end of his toothpick. "As a matter of fact, yeah. About the time you were shooting the Jeffers kid, another van was being bombed across town. We've had a rash of these bombings over the past three or four months now. Haven't you been reading the papers or watching the news?"

Nate flashed a startled look at Daniels, then slowly shook his head. "Well, they still tried to steal the tires, you know."

"Yeah, I know," Daniels replied, "but that doesn't give you the right to use deadly force."

"My feeling is if you get caught stealing, you deserve anything you get."

"I'm not quarreling with your feeling, son, just your use of a gun. Shit! Even I can't fire a gun in a non-life-threatening situation. Don't you know anything?"

Nate began to squirm and his hands clenched at the arms of the chair. "But I thought I had the right," he muttered.

Daniels flipped the pick to the other side of his mouth. "You know, of course, that boy you shot not only lost his kidney, but he's pretty well maimed for life."

Nate shook his head and shrugged his shoulders. "God, I'm so sorry I did that," he said. "I didn't mean to hurt him. If he had just stopped like I told him. I didn't think....Oh, I don't know," he sobbed. He looked down at his now clasped fingers, then up into the unwavering eyes of the Inspector.

Daniels stood up and walked over to the coffee pot. He poured a cup and offered it to Nate, who shook his head.

NOTHIN' BUT A BOB

10:10 AM January 17

Deputy DA Banks quickly leafed through the police reports delivered earlier this morning. He briefly went through each packet of papers and sorted them according to the class of crime. All of the driving offenses went into the basket to his left. The petty thefts and misdemeanor burglaries were plopped into the basket directly in front of him. The occasional drug case was automatically marked FELONY, no matter how small the score. The citizens liked to think those "filthy pushers" were being put away. Those cases went on the top shelf of his IN basket.

Banks pushed his chair away from his crowded desk, opened the middle drawer and put his feet up. This was a favorite position he assumed when reading something of interest, and this was pretty interesting—an attempted 187. The suspect had put it to the victim for tampering with a van. Frank began scribbling a few notes on his legal pad.

"Sixteen-year-old victim shot attempting to leave the scene of a crime. Victim lost kidney, maybe other internal injuries. Too soon to tell extent of damages. Victim will probably recover." Nothing but a BOB, he decided, flinging the folder in the "questionable felony" basket to his right.

8:15 AM January 31

David Michaelson stood outside Judge Margaret Caldwell's chambers. He recognized Frank Banks as he rounded the corner at the end of the corridor.

"Well, I'll be damned!" said Banks. "What brings you off the Corporate Hill and down to the Jungle where real people live?"

"It's been a long time, Frank. Say, when are you going to give up this...this...." he threw up his arms and rolled his eyes to the ceiling of the mint-green painted walls and mahogany woodwork of the back passage of the Municipal Court building.

Both men laughed good-naturedly. They had been classmates in law school. David had gone into the family firm and was now a successful corporate lawyer. Frank had opted for public service and joined the ranks of the district attorney's office. His secret hope was to become governor of the state once he caught that 'right case'.

"Frank, what can you tell me about your new lady judge?"

"What can I say? She's young, Black, and still green. If you
handle her right, you can get practically anything you want."

"Oh, yeah? How's that?"

"She was a political appointee, fresh out of the County Coun-
sel's office. What she knows about criminal law you could drop
in a gnat's ear and still hear an echo."

Both men chuckled again.

"That's good to hear because I've got the Walker case."

"He's the one who shot a kid about a van, right?"

"That's the one."

"Piece of cake. I'm appearing on that case and we're prepared
to offer a misdemeanor."

"On an attempted murder?" David asked incredulously.

"Yeah," he responded. "It ain't nothin' but a BOB."

Michaelson smiled at the pseudonym for Black On Black
crime. Things had not changed much.

1:30 PM February 16

Levy didn't like to talk to victims of violent crimes. They
always seemed so pathetic. But this case was a little bit different.
The victim had been in the midst of committing a crime himself
when the defendant shot him. There was the rub. The defendant
had made the mistake of shooting this kid. Levy shook his head.
Everybody turned up losers in a case like this.

"Albert Jeffers?"

The young man slowly stood up. A faint but pungent odor
accompanied him. Levy noted the little bulge on the youngster's
left side and made a mental note to keep his office door open.

After arranging himself as comfortably as possible in the visi-
tor's chair opposite the green metal desk, the boy managed an
almost bashful smile.

Levy began the interview exchanging pleasantries about the
new football league and what it would mean to the fans. He was
painfully aware that he was reluctant to speak of the reason this
kid now sat before him.

"Tell me, Albert," he took the plunge. "What were you and
your friends doing at the Walker residence the night you were
shot?"

Albert gulped and his hands began to shake.

145

"C'mon, Albert. You had to be there for a reason."

"I was just walking by and...."

Levy interrupted him. "You'll have to do better than that, Albert. When you get to the preliminary examination, Walker's attorney will cut you to ribbons if you try to shoot him that line of shit."

Albert lowered his head. "I know. The cops have already told me that, but," he suddenly looked at the probation officer, "if I tell the truth, I'll get myself in trouble."

"If you don't tell the truth, the man who shot you will walk and he'll think he has a license to kill anyone he finds on or near his property. Granted you were wrong to try to steal those tires; he still had no right to take a shot at you."

Levy stared at the boy who fidgeted on his seat, trying to decide how best to field the questions hurled at him.

"How do you feel about Walker and his having shot you?"

Albert frowned and twisted in his chair. "I hate that son of a bitch," he said softly. "You know what, Mr. Levy? I gotta wear this shit bag for the rest of my life," he said as he indicated the bulge at his side. "The doctor says I'm impotent and I can't have no kids, ever! You got any idea what that's gonna be like, Mr. Levy?"

3:15 PM February 28

The diminutive form of Margaret Caldwell was swamped by the massiveness of the chair she occupied in her recently acquired chambers. She was aware some felt she was not qualified for a judgeship, but she could give a little less than a damn.

Michaelson cleared his throat. Both the Judge and Banks looked in his direction.

"Your Honor, as the probation officer points out in his report, my client is young and the instant offense is his first arrest. Now I have spoken with the D.A. and he is prepared to offer a misdemeanor if the Court agrees."

The Judge glanced at Banks.

"That's correct, Your Honor. We don't feel the merits of this case warrant a felony charge."

"Exactly what merits are you considering, Mr. Banks?"

"Well, Your Honor, the victim was caught stealing from the

defendant, therefore, provocation exists."

"Yes, Your Honor," Michaelson interrupted, "my client was merely trying to protect his property when this unfortunate incident occurred."

"So the ends justify the means?"

"Er, not exactly, Your Honor," Banks said, risking a nervous glance at Michaelson. "It's just that it might prove difficult to get a jury to convict when they learn the victim was partially to blame for this."

"Am I to understand you are only interested in your conviction record?"

"Of course not, Your Honor. But in this time of fiscal embarrassment...."

"Cut the crap, Banks. What's the real reason you don't want to pursue this matter?"

"Beg pardon?" Banks stalled.

"I don't stutter, Mr. Banks. Just answer the question," the Judge said. A shade of displeasure had crept into her demeanor.

"Oh, we're prepared to press forward, Your Honor, but it seems unfair to ruin this defendant's life with a felony conviction."

"Is there no consideration for the victim, or am I to understand we are to look at this as just another BOB?" asked the Judge.

Frank Banks blanched. David Michaelson turned scarlet to pale.

"Yes, gentlemen," said the Judge. "I am well aware Black On Black crime is referred to as a BOB. You can rest assured in my Court, however, justice will not be balanced on the scales of indifference. Mr. Michaelson prepare your client for preliminary examination."

Michaelson slowly began to regain his color. "Thank you, Your Honor," he mumbled.

"Mr. Banks, if you are not prepared to submit a case based on merit, I strongly suggest you find yourself another line of work."

Frank opened his mouth as it to speak, then changed his mind.

"Is there a problem, Mr. Banks?"

"No, Your Honor. There is no problem whatsoever."

Judge Margaret Caldwell donned her black robe.

NOTHIN' BUT A BOB

8:45 AM March 21

The Honorable Margaret Caldwell leafed through the probation report. The defendant stood at attention next to his attorney, David Michaelson.

"You have read the probation report?" Judge Caldwell asked.

"We have, Your Honor," said Michaelson.

"Are you prepared for sentencing?"

"Yes, we are, Your Honor," Michaelson answered for his client.

The Judge glanced down at her sheaf of papers, then tamped them into a neat stack.

"Mr. Jeffers," the Judge called, looking out over the Court room.

Jeffers rose from his seat just beyond the railing. The Judge beckoned him forward.

"Before I pass judgment, is there anything you wish to say, Mr. Jeffers?"

Jeffers looked over at Nate Walker, who returned his gaze. Each took the measure of the other, regretting those few minutes that had altered their lives.

Nate glared at Jeffers, taking in the angry eyes and hostile bearing of the youth, three years his junior, who now faced him. He saw the slight bulge at the boy's left side and remembered the missing kidney and talk about impotence.

Jeffers returned the stare, calling forth the hatred he had nurtured over the past several weeks. He thrust aside thoughts of his involvement that created this situation, unwilling to accept responsibility for his behavior.

"I just want to see justice done, Your Honor," Jeffers said softly.

"Mr. Jeffers," she began, "had not Mr. Walker shot you, you would probably be facing the Juvenile Court on charges of tampering with a vehicle. Instead, you are now the victim who has suffered pain and great personal loss. As the result of your criminal behavior, I must sentence Mr. Walker. I'm sure you can see this is a no-win situation and that makes this hearing all the more difficult for those concerned."

Judge Caldwell paused to take a sip of water.

"Mr. Walker, I have pondered your case for the past several

weeks. You were under the grave misapprehension that you had
the right to use whatever means necessary to protect your property. By now I'm sure you realize that we are not living in the Old
West where the .45 was law."

"Yes, Your Honor," said Walker.

"Now the probation officer has recommended leniency, citing
Mr. Jeffers' criminal activity as a mitigating factor, as well as
your lack of prior record, employed status, and youth. Probation
is granted for three years. You will make restitution to Mr. Jeffers
for his medical expenses. I am imposing a one-year jail sentence
which will be suspended pending your successful completion of
probation."

Judge Caldwell raised her gavel and almost as an afterthought
said, "Good luck, gentlemen."

JUAN PEDRO'S HIGH DESTINY
Virginia Ruiz Seiden

"As a favor, Señor Presidente, do not go today beyond the park. It is not that we would curtail your liberty. It is that we fear for your life," said the guard to Juan Pedro with a respectful bow.

Juan noticed that he wore no gun. "How do they expect to protect me without guns?" he asked himself as he obediently returned from the direction from which he had come. Was this part of the system he had been expounding to the people of his country for so many years? It seemed ironic that the military should be the first to understand...If only the nation would do the same...If only the entire world were willing to make the change... to stand aside and let the unseen Power operate, then Juan Pedro would be free to return to public life. Free to make useful mistakes and pay for them, but not by facing the firing squad. But the stupidity of divided interests, the agony and madness of misunderstanding, the labyrinth of red tape where bright plans entangled, rotted and soiled the soul of man....

In the meantime, patience, caution...and compromise. The hour of final victory was bound to come. In fact, it was already coming with the acceleration of time.

This restlessness Juan felt today—wasn't that a sure sign? And also the sadness he'd seen in his mother's sweet, dark eyes. She had not come to see him in a very long while. Juan wondered why.

"Just this once and only for a few minutes. There's no private phone in the Palace," he whispered to the guard after returning to the gate.

"Mister President...your wishes are orders...but it's visiting time. You should stay near the main gate...please, Mister President...?"

Such servility....Perhaps the poor man knew Juan Pedro's

influence was growing and wanted to preserve his post. But Juan could not lose even a minute arguing. There were so many demands on his time. He turned about face and began to walk back, hunched up like an old man, with his hands clasped behind his back. His blue eyes were lifted to the sky.

The high trees were full of birds and the new leaves were a tender green. Was it spring again? Time certainly flew by. Years went past so fast. He didn't care. He loved this park. He spent most of his time here walking to and fro. That helped him to concentrate and gave him a fine appetite. He was going to need strength to develop his ambitious plan. Meanwhile he must submit, in every detail, to a magnificently complicated life in the Presidential Palace, while an impostor lived in the castle by the lake and gave orders to men born deaf.

Someday, however, they'd all hear the Voice which directed Juan Pedro to accept this confinement. Glory would come when the time was ripe. But for now, while the secret preparations went on, he must have peace. And the way to peace was dualism and compromise.

He had discovered dualism when his family decided with loving accord to leave him in the care of secret underground sympathizers—that is, to throw him out of their cramped central apartments. By doing this they had helped him more than they knew. Juan Pedro's sleeping quarters were now the best in the Palace, the most modern and comfortable. Such privacy! He even had a shower of his own. Those outside the Palace who still opposed him might murmur that his exile and seclusion in such luxury went against his former preachments for equality and democracy, but Juan knew why he was here. His enemies had sought to destroy him, but the unseen Power had provided a refuge, time and opportunity to complete the blueprint for his vast undertaking. He was, therefore, satisfied. His only suffering was in not seeing more often the only person who really understood him, the one who had never been afraid of him and therefore had never opposed him. She who had never blamed him or belittled his ambitions. What kept his mother away so long? Had she gone on to prepare the way? If so, her favorite son must be ready to follow soon. The supposition excited Juan; it made him decide to...

The necklace of high spiked fence which surrounded the Park ended at another beautiful wrought iron gate. Here a second guard detained him. Juan bowed in submission. The walk that led to the Palace was full of civilians taking the air before midday dinner, and it was important for the President to give them all a good example.

Outside the gate a significant car stopped—significant because the two men and two women inside were looking at Juan and smiling. Juan looked intently at those four people. Although none of them were his mother, they somehow brought the memory of his mother with them. Their sudden appearance made Juan Pedro's heart beat faster with excitement and joy mixed with sorrow at the thought that his time might have finally come.

"Mister President, you may walk out and see your brothers and sisters. They are waiting for you in the car," said the guard. And everyone, all his aides and even his enemies in the Palace, came out of hiding and gazed while the gate opened and Juan walked out with great dignity.

He fell first into his older sister Victoria's arms.

"I haven't seen you for years. When did you arrive from the United States?" He didn't wait for an answer.

"There was a time when I myself wanted to live on the other side of the border, remember?"

"Yes, but your followers in Mexico...I mean, we could not afford...and the treatments take time...besides, remember my husband is an American...."

"I know. Americans are too proud to admit that their salvation depends on Mexico's salvation and on supporting me. So going to the U.S.A. at that time would have worked against the cause. I will cross the border later, when it means progress for all..."

His sister's dark eyes were full of tears, but those belonged to the outside world. Juan had nothing to do with them.

He turned to Elena, the younger sister. "And you, weren't you living in Guaymas? What are you doing here?" he asked. His sister's big blue eyes were pools where two babies were drowning. But they were also part of the world outside the Palace.

Gerardo, the younger brother with the balding head who was always joking, embraced him laughing. "You look fine, Señor Presidente," he said.

Juan had seen him often and also Eduardo, the older one with the bushy, angry eyebrows, who was always so gentle and kind. Both came regularly to the Palace to bring him pocket money and gifts. But the girls...

"Why did my sisters come from so far...leaving their own families?" he asked, naive as always. "Is this some kind of special holiday?"

Instead of answering, his brothers and sisters patted his back, kissed his cheeks and finally pulled him into the car, remarking about his new beard, but all the time watching his innocent blue eyes made solemn by years of brooding. They told him his greying beard made him look important, and he joked, "I am now the father of you all!" The muscles of his cheeks hurt as he laughed. A smile was rare in him, but laughter was obsolete. But today he was very, very happy. He saw no reason for the others to cry.

"Mother is ill," they explained.

"Yes, I know. She hasn't come to the Palace for weeks."

"Yes. But Juan, this time it is serious. She may die."

Juan's heart began to beat wildly. It was the awaited sign that his High Destiny was in sight.

"But tell us about you...the doctors say your health is better than it has ever been."

A white-clad young man who had been standing at attention nearby leaned forward and whispered, "He's almost well enough to go home."

"No!" said Juan quickly. "The work is not completed. Some people in Mexico still don't want me for president." He blushed like a girl. "They still don't believe in me."

"Never mind. We believe in you," said Victoria.

"And we're proud of you," Elena said promptly.

"Everyone tells us about the wonderful way you conduct yourself," said Victoria, "how disciplined you are."

Juan sighed. His brows knitted and his throat contracted with anguish. "Yes, but how long...how long will this preparation go on...?" Suddenly, as he realized that he would not have his mother's visits any more, the wheel of time had slowed down. Compromise had become a strain. "We must hurry things up It's important," he said. "When my time comes you can expect to recoup what father lost during the revolution."

His family tensed. "Don't start worrying again," said Victoria. "You're doing fine. Everything is all right. Just thank God. That's what we all have to do to be happy, you know."

"Life isn't easy for any one of us, either," said Elena, her sweet voice like a kitten's whine. Juan turned to her. Was this the sister Mamacita said looked like him?

"And how are you?" he said with sudden attention.

"I have to have an operation," Elena replied.

"And you?" he asked Victoria, with a forced smile.

"I have to have a divorce." The two women looked at each other and laughed ruefully.

Juan shook his head with a sad expression. "Too bad," he said. But he thought, "Good riddance." He was ashamed and confused by his duality. But that was wisdom. Duplicity and compromise.

"Did you get my last letter from Guaymas?" Elena asked.

"Yes."

"Why didn't you answer me?"

Juan's face twisted with impatience. "Frankly, little sister...I have such little time..."

The sisters and brothers exchanged a quick grin.

"What do you do all day?" Victoria asked.

Her brother Gerardo answered for Juan. "They tell me he gets up at dawn, prays, does his exercises, showers....After breakfast he takes a walk while meditating on important problems." Accentuating his serious Buster Keaton expression he added, "I suppose he might give a few orders before dinnertime."

"I don't...I play chess..." Juan announced happily. "Everything is done here without my having to give orders."

"I'm so glad...so glad. Things are much better for you then," said his older sister. "...Aren't they?"

"Oh, yes," said Juan. "Though of course important matters have to be kept a secret...like how our fortune was lost."

"You've got it all wrong," interrupted Eduardo in a soft voice, though his brows knitted fiercely. "We never saw grandfather's fortune. Father had nothing when he joined the revolution. But never mind that."

"We don't talk about it any more. It all happened long ago, and we don't understand it very well," said Victoria, smiling. "Besides, we are not doing so badly any more, all of us. Mamacita has lacked nothing since father died. Thank God for that."

"Here's some money for you," said Eduardo, giving it to him.

"That's too much," Juan replied. "Give me only a couple of pesos and some change for the telephone."

"But surely there is something else you need?" Elena asked.

"Yes....What can we do to help?" asked Victoria.

"Help? You mean the Great Cause?"

"No, we mean help *you*," said Elena.

"Your sweater is all torn at the elbows," Victoria remarked.

"I was going to ask you," said the older brother, "what happened to the sweater we gave you last Christmas?"

Juan shrugged his shoulders.

"You didn't rent it again, did you?"

"Rent it?" asked Victoria, surprised.

"Yes, I rent things out when I need cash," Juan said proudly. "I got one peso for my pillow for those three months none of you came to the Palace." He was talking to his brothers.

"You have no idea the dreadful things which happened to both of us during that time," Gerardo explained. "I lost my job. Our car got stolen. Nivea had a new baby...then the whole family got the flu."

He looked at his older brother, who was mumbling something, his bushy brows gnarled. "Eduardo here was fighting a drinking problem."

"Working too hard and too long at a boring job...and then Rosita died," said Eduardo, his tortured eyes on the floor.

"Rosita?"

"His oldest girl," Victoria said in a strangled voice. "The beautiful one with the long black hair who used to put on skits and recite poems on Mamacita's saintday. But you still have many nieces and nephews. At least a dozen," she said brightly.

"I never see them," said Juan Pedro.

"That's not true. You've seen all but the last one. You were at our house last Christmas...and my oldest girls have come to see you. How could you forget?" said Eduardo.

"Well, you know...I have important things on my mind... Oh, just a moment, all of you...see? The crowd is gone from the gate. They are gone inside. That means dinner time. You'll have to excuse me. It's important to be punctual..." He got out of the car. "Come inside and wait, if you like."

"We can't...we'll be leaving soon...we left Mamacita alone with the nurses and cousin Carmen. You go...we'll wait for you in the car, if you don't take long."

The guards bowed as Juan, chatting amiably, joined the group that was going for chow.

"You see? He's happy here," said one of the brothers, "and no danger that he will throw himself under a trolley car again. They don't run this far." He was looking at Elena and Victoria, who assented. Then Victoria spoke.

"Shall we take him to the hospital to see Mamacita? She asked about him."

"We better not. It might upset him. Anyway, she won't recognize him now."

"Yes, let's tell him only when it's all over."

"I'm glad to see he has peace of mind at last," said Victoria, sighing.

"Greater peace of mind than we have, I'm sure," said Gerardo.

"The guards, the nurses, the inmates—everyone seems to like him," observed Elena.

"Of course they do. He doesn't have any more fits and he doesn't give anyone any trouble. Actually he's perfect. Do you know what he said to me one day after the doctors praised him? He said that one day after he took his daily shower and paid the money he owed one of the guards, it came to him as a revelation that the reason he had been elected to the high position of president was that the people recognized him as the cleanest and the most honest man in Mexico."

The four of them laughed until tears came to their eyes, and they felt relaxed and happy being together. Then the older sister said, "I'd like to give him something."

"Yes, but what?" one of the brothers asked. "Anything we give him will only get stolen...like the sweater. That's why we cannot give him too much cash."

"Here he comes."

Juan approached them, placid and satisfied. "I couldn't eat, knowing that you have to get back to Mamacita," he said. "So good-bye."

"We want to give you a present," said the sisters, embracing him.

"I almost forgot," said one of the brothers. "We brought you the alarm clock you asked for." And he began to unwrap a package.

"Oh. That was in the winter, because it wasn't easy to wake up. I don't need it any more. I wake up with the sun. Take it back. It looks expensive. You probably need the money more than I do."

"It's not expensive, but it's good quality. Keep it in your drawer and don't show it to anyone."

Juan took the present. "Gracias."

"What else do you want?"

"Nothing, really."

"Sure you don't want more cash?"

"No. I charge everything I buy at the corner store. They let me walk there sometimes. The man there knows me. Soon everyone in Mexico will know me. I will have good credit everywhere. Here is the list of my debts, if you want to pay them."

Gerardo took the list and read: "For cigarettes, 85 centavos; matches, 20 centavos; chewing gum, 25 centavos; lost on a bet to El Señor Dominguez, 50 centavos; lost playing chess, 60 centavos."

Juan Pedro pocketed the coins he was given, and remained at the gate of the Sanatorium to wave at his family as they drove away. How complicated was their life...so many children and struggles and illnesses and anguish...so much detail and red tape and stupidity and madness....And above all, he thought compassionately as he joined his friends who played chess, no time at all for the things in life that really mattered...

The tall eucalyptus trees whispered tenderly. A butterfly smiled as it danced in front of his eyes. The sun shone cheerfully and simply upon everyone.

In his pocket he felt the weight of the alarm clock. Someday, he thought peacefully, it would ring in vain...the day when he would have crossed the border and ended dualism and compromise forever.

MAUDIE
Marlin Spike Werner

The afternoon sun warmed the hills. The grass in the meadow adjoining the graveyard stood tall and bronze against the evergreens beyond. The Great Smoky Mountains were clad in russets, golds and deep green. Their massiveness hovered over the village of Fawns' Glen embracing it with a protective intimacy. A lone bee explored the blossoms which were banked alongside the raw earth of a newly prepared grave.

Len Crawford threaded his way among the cars which crowded the road, the roadside, and the parking lot. He was a newcomer to Fawns' Glen. Thirty and balding, he felt stiff and alien in his well-tailored tan suit, an urban intruder. Again he congratulated himself on his decision to become a small-town lawyer instead of joining his dad's firm in St. Louis. He liked the people, the mountains, the flowers, the smells and sounds of Jackson County, North Carolina. He liked the slower pace of living, three-day weekends, and fishing with his neighbors. Nonetheless, he approached the events of this day with a feeling of awkwardness; for this was his first country funeral.

He nodded to the farm folk as he rubbed shoulders with them. They were dressed in their Sunday best, the sun-scorched skin of their faces glowing above their collars.

Ahead, the Fawns' Glen Baptist Church was a raw, three-story cube of yellow brick—a harsh functional structure without the benefit of a steeple, and he wondered whether the lovely country churches of New England had begun as such ungainly boxes. Perhaps they'd mellowed as their parishioners prospered. Road dust dulled the leaves of the shrubbery and the wildflowers. The walls of the chapel returned the heat of that same sun which gave vitality to the surrounding forests and those rare and precious bottom-lands which were wide and flat enough to bear crops.

158

The streams of people converged with many murmurings and noddings. With them, Len passed through the front door, and then they spread delta-like into the pews.

He stood for a minute, observing the chapel. The pulpit and altar rail were banked with wine-red sprays of dogwood leaves, their berries scarlet, highlighted by a ray of sun coming through the plain glass of the west-facing window beyond the altar. Chrysanthemums were banked to either side. This was not a Sunday morning, however; it was Saturday afternoon.

Three days back, Maude Watson had quietly drawn her last breath, and now was the time for farewells.

Still perspiring from the sun, Len took a seat at the back. On his left were two polished boys, the redhead next to him about ten years old, the towhead beyond maybe nine. Their hair was still wet and freshly combed, and they sat there red-faced and subdued. From time to time they glanced cow-eyed at the stern-faced heavy-set lady on their left. On Len's right, an obese woman in a dress with a purple floral print squeezed in. She smelled as if she had spilled rose perfume all over herself. With the fan in her right hand, she pumped little gusts of the heavy scent in his direction.

He felt conspicuous among these strangers. He thought he might be seen as an intruder looking with fascination into the private softness of the Watson family's grief. He was not only unused to funerals, he was also uncomfortable with deeply-felt emotions. He had never met Mrs. Maude Watson, and was here only because her son Robert had invited him. Robert was his first friend and neighbor in his new surroundings.

Len looked about the room. The guests were quiet and serious. Occasionally he saw an eye glistening with unspilled tears. The pews filled and the newcomers spread to the side aisles and along the back wall, and now he saw Robert and Faye Watson at the altar rail, responding with shy gratitude to the well-wishers. Though the windows were open, the air was still. Len picked up scents of moth crystals, pig and horse manure, cheese-making, hay, ham fat, and kitchen condiments.

He knew that Robert's mother, the late Maude Watson, had been bedridden for ten years with Huntington's chorea, but he'd never seen her. She had lived at the home of Robert's brother, William. Her mind had failed many years ago and since then she had vegetated like a parked automobile, motor running, but without its driver. Who knew when, in all that time, the *real* Maude Watson had departed. And now the church was brimming with more mourners than Fawns' Glen had people. What kind of person was this Maude Watson that her fame retained such a hold on folks for so many years?

Len turned to the lady on his left. "My name's Crawford."

"Mine's Kimball," she replied, "Mizz Prentice Kimball, pleased to meet you."

"It's nice the Watsons have so many friends."

"Oh, we ain't friends," implying that others had come with her, "but they got themselves one preachin' parson for this funeral an' we wouldn't miss him for anything. That Delos Hoyles will do Mrs. Watson proud for sure, yessir!"

Len could barely make out Robert and Faye up front. Robert's face was all freckles and his wavy blonde hair was sun-bleached. Faye blushed uncomfortably with all the attention they were getting. Other members of the family had joined them, William, Julus, Gillud, Newton, and Edith, and inlaws like Glenn Worley and Talmadge Leopard.

Suddenly the murmur of voices and the fidgeting stopped. The people in the pews sat down.

At the altar stood Parson Delos Hoyles.

For a moment a hummingbird stopped at the northwest window, wings droning, and was gone.

Delos Hoyles was a florid-faced heavy-set man. He looked imposing in his black suit and tie. His hair, even lighter in color than Robert's, was thin, allowing the sunburned crown of his head to shine through. His cheeks were plump, he had an overbite, and yet above all he had an earnestness that commanded attention. Pearls of perspiration formed on his brow, and he daubed them off with a large white handkerchief which he periodically took from his coat pocket.

Silence. Hoyles' hands gripped the sides of the lectern, knuckles white. How serious he looked—how imbued with importance! The silence seemed to hum. All eyes were on the parson.

The good man looked purposefully first to his right, then left, then down the center aisle. Len felt impaled by that gaze—committed to the events of this day, wedded to the course of things and to this community at his elbows.

Hoyles kept his silence dramatically. Then the good man began to shake. He turned his face to look up, up, beyond the roofbeams to the Heavens themselves.

In a baritone voice which shook with its burden of emotion, and so quietly that Len had to strain to understand him, he said, "Poor Maudie." His voice quavered. The last syllable was inflected as if in those two words he were asking, "Why, Lord, why she, why me, why this human condition with sorrow, pain and death? Poor, poor Maudie."

He gave a soft sob and dabbed his eyes with his handkerchief.

"Oh Lord, in Thy Divine Providence to give and to take away, you have gathered our Maudie to your own. How very empty we feel." His voice broke as his anguish overwhelmed him, and he sobbed into his handkerchief, his red face turning almost purple with emotion.

There was a suspenseful silence as he fought to contain his grief.

The sense of loss was contagious. Len felt it and wondered at the unfamiliar emotion. He watched and listened and felt a magic in the silence of his fellow mourners who now leaned forward, scarcely breathing, intent upon Delos Hoyles' every word. He listened, and he felt ashamed. How often have I made fun of country preachers, of parsons whose flocks live by the soil and the dictates of the seasons, and to whom life and death are frequent, urgent, immediate, and have to be transcended for life to continue!

"Such was her Fate in this life," Hoyles continued, "that she was to spend her last ten years more dead than alive in her affliction. Take kindly to her, Lord; she were a good woman." Tears spilled down his cheeks.

"Poor Maudie! Dear, lovely Maudie! Good wife and mother, friend and neighbor, how clearly I recall your figure on the porch, rockin' in your chair, stringin' up the beans to dry and laughin' and singin', and it's those happy days which I cherish. And before all that, there was tiny Maudie, born into this world of promise, hope and joy. And there was little Maudie in her Sunday pinafore, laughing and romping in the meadow with the spring wildflowers. My daddy said she were the twinkling star of the whole parish!"

By now the tears streamed unashamedly down Pastor Hoyles' cheeks. Len heard sobs and sniffles, and glancing at Mrs. Kimball, saw that her face too was streaked with tears.

"And then there were her first blossom of womanhood, beautiful, happy, loving and loveable. Her marriage and startin' up her own family."

Pastor Hoyles stopped speaking. It was abrupt. His face became resolute, his jaw set, his eyebrows knitted. Len held his breath. The silence stretched on and he wondered what was to come.

"GONE!" Hoyles shouted, "—GONE! All gone!—Hopes—and dreams—and love—and laughter—all gone!"

It was a voice of anger and outrage, of passion and sorrow.

"Oh Lord, can you *ever* fill this emptiness!?"

Delos Hoyles clutched at his heart and sobbed.

Len heard Mrs. Kimball crying openly, and then the old man just ahead. Everywhere he looked he saw heaving chests, tears, handkerchiefs. And then he felt smitten by it too. Tears welled up in his eyes. A great well of feeling opened in his chest, and he was overwhelmed with grief. The little detachment he had left was pushed to one side to peer at him in bewilderment, and he gave himself over to profound feelings of loss and heartbreak.

Maudie had departed forever without Len Crawford's ever having known her. As he joined his tears with those around him, he felt that the whole world mourned the passing of dear Maudie Watson, and he began to be aware of something else. He was crying for all the Maudie Watsons, for all lost hopes and dying dreams, for broken hearts and loves lost, for his own life and his own death.

When the sermon was concluded, Len joined the family at the graveside. The service was simple and brief. The casket was lowered, " . . .ashes to ashes . . ." and it was over. Neighbors came around and introduced themselves to Len, offering invitations of hospitality. They gave their respects to the Watsons and went their respective ways.

Len looked beyond the many tombstones to the meadow. The sky was God's-eye blue and the grasses winter gold. The evening shadow of the mountain crept across the back fence, and honking far overhead, a string of geese beat their way southward. A scarf of hickory smoke hung on the air.

Little Connie came running up to her granddaddy. Len watched as Robert picked her up and she threw her arms around his neck in a hug. His eyes still glistening with tears, Robert smiled. Joyously and with a look of fulfillment, he hugged his precious granddaughter. "That were a fine funeral!" he said, looking proud.

Len, a man without children, looked on with envy. It was not only through the days and seasons, but also through the births and deaths that a community measures time, and he saw the succession of generations as a stream. Maudie's life, Robert's, his own, and Connie's, were as eddies, rivulets and spray—fleeting features in the river of life's passage.

He returned to his car, reflecting that he had witnessed a process of healing.

A hawk wheeled in the lingering sunglow above Buck's Knob. Ned Grover's mare scratched her neck on an old oak tree. A gray fence lizard froze against a post. Loosening his collar, Len felt at peace with himself in unfamiliar ways, and with renewed energy he whistled up a tune.

THE ART OF ACTING NORMAL
Nina Zeitler Clark

I can tell it's January because it's back again; it seems to be setting a pattern for itself. Summers are fairly benign, Septembers may find me digging compost into the garden, but by Christmas the pain in my hands will have begun, and soon after comes tendinitis, exhaustion, and other symptoms of body breakdown in a disease called rheumatoid arthritis.

Shoulder joints grate against themselves as I struggle into a blazer, pull up a zipper. Feet, now too tender to walk barefoot except on thick carpeting, send me to the closet for shoes of soft leather on crepe-cushioned soles. By March, typing will be an ordeal, even on the smooth electric, to say nothing of getting a sweater over my head, opening a car door, or slicing a carrot.

The worst part, and yet the most wonderful, is that the pain is not visible; without a careful look at my hands, or my deliberate movements, I seem Perfectly Well.

Once, in a restaurant, someone clapped me roughly on the arm: "I haven't seen you for awhile, how have you been, you look wonderful!" they said without waiting for answers.

Witnessing this, Edna, comrade and companion, asked later, "Would it help if they could see it?"

"Yes," I replied instantly. "I'd like a bandage around my head."

Nights of pulling up from my bed to search through the medicine chest for some chemical relief; mornings of frustrated sobbing as I try to fasten my clothes, or reach up for some sugar; the small indignities of using styrofoam cups at home because they are lighter, of lifting a mug or glass with both hands when eating out; mercifully, these do not show on the outside.

("Come to the potluck," urges a friend, and I reply, "Of course, love to!" At home, I survey the kitchen: Forget my specialty—

baked beans with bacon-onion overlay—the flat casserole dish is too heavy. A green salad, maybe, with easy-to-slice tomatoes, in a plastic bowl.)

At a party there is no compassion when I ask, "Will you open this fliptop can for me?" or "Will you pour me a cup of coffee?" Unusual requests, bringing odd looks, because I appear So Healthy.

Even friends who know cannot comprehend, and why should they? How can they perceive unless they live it? And would I want them really to know, if I could; wouldn't that change one more of the cherished, still intact qualities of living that means I am Normal in a society that worships Normality?

And so I must accept this annual enemy within my body, one that retreats each year, but only after destroying a few more of my walls, invading a bit more of my shoring, leaving more rubble piled against the bulwarks of my defenses.

But every night, before my restless sleep, The Question:

Will my act give out before my body?

BREATHE DEEPLY
Clara Robbin

So breathe deeply. What's death but the end of breath?

What does one do when words like loneliness and grief become clichés?

Talk to me. Say something.

Which is the real world?

Life. Long, melancholy afternoons, nights and times between wellwisher's visits. Or where you are. I can't accept your death as a final separation.

Shall I say, "He's not dead. He's just away."? Shall I think of you as the same? I miss the friendship and companionship I cherished through the years.

Your absence, yes, your absence leaves hollows, resoundingly empty spaces.

Can you hear me?

Are life and death opposites?

Answer me. From where you are, how do you cope with loneliness and empty spaces? Can you feel and touch?

How do you fathom it? What is it like? Is the body irrelevant?

Do you wake in the morning? Go to sleep at night?

Do you know where you are going? Which path to follow? Or did you take the ultimate step into another world, no paths, no doors. A final severance. You gave your whole self away, dropped into a black hole!

Shall I think of you as the man I knew?

Do you have dreams?

Since you are not here to share, *dreams* don't come readily, to me, the dreamer.

The other night I *was* graced with a dream.

Your velvet voice came through the door with a laughing, humorous chuckle. You said, "Ha, I fooled them, just walked out of that jail. Freedom, at last, on my own terms, too." Looking at me you said, "Did you know me as a child?" Before I could answer, you dissolved, vanished.

The dream lingered on. I conjured up the curly headed, swarthy child. Spindly legged Izzy. The large, dark, amber eyes whose questioning, troubled look I still see in my old friend sitting before me.

Images, memories and stories. Izzy, a sickly child, confined frequently to bed rest with bouts of bronchitis. Often absent from school. Accepting mother's ministrations of mustard plasters and special treats. Looking out the window, watching children at play. Reading books a teacher gave him or those stocked up on his frequent trips to the library.

The skill of reading he acquired early, in spite of the interruptions in his school attendance.

Thus, he watched, read and indulged in an inner dialogue. He lived an inner life enriched by books and loving care. Undemonstrative, contemplative. No anger, no fights.

When he did come to school it was as a shining light. Editor of the school paper, leader of poetry sessions and theater groups, valedictorian.

A writer was born!

The reverie ended. Or did it?

Now I see you wave your hand and wander into the unknown.

Life or death. There must be something more to the other side. Who can tell me if not you?

The end of the road must have a path leading somewhere, to Eternity, perhaps? What's Eternity? Where is it?

Is death really life veiled in secrecy and mystery, or is it life obliterated, negated?

Questions, questions. No answers.

In my dream world, I see you as a river rushing along with no thought of where to . . . .

Can you hear me?

Or is the sound of silence all you know?

You seem to be visible and invisible at the same time.

Did you say you are on a different planet? Do you meet other souls? All I remember is the physical you.

So back to dreams and myths. Dreams and myths bring us back to reality.

The tall, beautiful, curly headed boy at my side. Walking hand in hand in the Old City of Jerusalem, the moon shining through on the cobble stones. A careless, sensual boy accepting love as his due, whispering love words in my ear.

Where are you now?

Is your soul or spirit floating free in space?

I see you as a bird with a built-in compass that guides you.

You are part of space, time and air, floating over streams, oceans and trees.

Floating free, connected to everything, only bodyless.

Lend me a wing so I may join you.

Could I dream myself floating on cloud nine, meeting you in space, or Eternity? In the astral world?

The physical you I see before me.

No matter where you sat in a room, the place became the center stage. All the people, your audience.

You'd crook one leg over the other, pick up your pipe, knock it against the heel of your shoe, press tobacco in the bowl with one finger, spill some on the rug.

Attention getters. Effective and heart warming.

Do I want to be brought back to reality?

I can't accept your death.

When I hear the key in a door,

Oh, Ed has come home.

Or, I turn to you, "Eddie, how do you spell this word? Did you read this story?" On and on. I can't accept your absence.

I need you to show me the way out of this dead end.

I've lost my way. Show me the path to follow.

Is death the end of being, the end of craving, loving?

I've lost my way. Answer me.

Wish I could believe in the mystery of an afterlife, or pre-existence, reincarnation.

Is it true that nothing really ever dies?

Why do I always say *We*, or *Our* house?

I need a new way of looking at life and death. Your absence is so ever present, yet I can't accept your death.

They say Time, a year. It takes a year.

But every day is a year.

They say, "Death is not just coming to an end, it's a beginning."

They say, "The passing of one is the birth of another."

Is death a reality, a cyclical nature of life? Can one choose how to live, how to die?

You come to me only when I think of you as the special person in my life.

When you came home from the Navy, with a bundle of writings. Good newspaper copy stories.

The Left rejected your writing. Others rejected you for your left affiliations.

So you gave up writing, became a business man, and made money.

Your gift of making friends led you from one venture to another. Surplus war materials, a building contractor, real estate, etc..

You brought home new friends, the clerk at City Hall, the building engineer, a maintenance man, all became lifelong friends. And women, many women. A life well lived.

Your availability and gentle humor attracted women. Responsibility for children you left to me. But they loved your permissiveness, your light touch. They loved you for the gentle support and humor.

Rummaging through the clutter of the years, I came across letters, some from Israel, some from the Navy. I discovered a new dimension in you.

To me, in 1933, from Israel: *"It's Saturday morning, I feel just like nothing, not sad, or glad, good or bad, just empty, lazy, idle.*

"Am thinking of Saul treading on graves of dead lovers. May call the book 'Birth'" (*Birth* was published fifty years later, one month before Ed's death.)

And from the Navy in 1944. A letter to twelve year old Danny.

"Had your letter, Dan. Your account of the meetings was so good. I felt as though I've been there. I'm immensely pleased that you like your job and appreciate Saul and the printing. Tell me more of the smell of printer's ink."

"A bonanza. Received four letters today.
One from Tamara and from Dan.

Lots of heart-warming news.

Dan's chicken project was new to me. I'm going to watch it with interest.

Science! I see it all now, what was lacking in our previous ventures was science.

But Clara's remark, 'how you haven't lost a single chicken since I left,' cut me to the quick.

"By the way, Tamara, do you like the poems I sent you? I sure like yours. I have another for you. Here it is . . . .

"Clara, your letters are truly wonderful and made me feel that you really are quite a treasure for such a small package. I wonder where you acquired so much wisdom. And the letter in answer to my jealous one was certainly a good spanking, but it made me chuckle. I take it all back. I hope you're not too old to recognize jealousy? You always did see the good things in me."

Some day I may make a book of your letters. Reading them brings you into the room speaking with your voice.

I wish you hadn't left so gracefully and unexpectedly.

Now, dreams of earthquakes.

Dreams of dead-end streets, street after street after street. Getting lost in strange yet familiar places, calling your name in the darkness of the night, waking to total emptiness.

Help us be always hopeful, garden of the Spirit.

Without darkness

Nothing comes to birth.

Without light

Nothing flowers.

They say, "When your lover leaves, a woman can enjoy living alone."

Not this woman, and what kind of living? What *time* in your life?

So, breathe deeply, what's death but the end of breath?

DIFFERENT STROKES
Ed Robbin

I was strolling in north Oakland one spring day in 1968, looking at buildings and thinking about making an investment in real estate, when I came upon an elderly lady sitting in a rocking chair in front of a stucco house. She was doing a crossword puzzle. Looking over her shoulder, I supplied 'paleolithic'.

This won me points, and I soon discovered that she wanted to sell the house. She showed me around. Within a few days I had bought the property with a thousand dollars down.

The main building was a rambling structure, at least fifty years old, with a high hedge, peeling paint and a general air of neglect. It was peculiarly designed. The downstairs had several small bedrooms off a corridor with a shared kitchen and bath. Up a set of rickety steps was a rather large one-bedroom flat with its own kitchen and bath.

In the rear was a small attached studio apartment and a separate garage. At the back of the lot there was a charming thatched cottage.

I rented the cottage to a lovely young woman who painted its interior in bright, warm colors. She also sanded and finished the floors, painted the eaves of the front porch with psychedelic rainbow designs and created an interesting patio in the rear with murals on the fence.

The studio in the back was occupied by a bearded fellow who worked as a librarian on a mobile truck and spent his leisure in meditation and the study of eastern religions.

These tenants were fairly stable, but the rooms and the apartment in front had renters coming and going, passing their places on to friends without even letting me know. Also, there were whole colonies of cats and dogs.

I was a non-intervening landlord who saw little reason for

171

raising rents, so I was accepted as a human being and found it easy to drop in on the place frequently.

Part of my reason was to collect the rent, which sometimes came in dribs and drabs. Sometimes, instead of money, it was paid in goods or services. For example, I soon had quite a few 'god's eyes' on my walls, and I never had to worry about my copy of the *Berkeley Barb*. Sometimes the tenants worked for me, painting a room or trimming a hedge, instead of paying cash. But one way or another these people did pay the rent, and they never tried to hide or avoid me.

The main reason I came around often was because I enjoyed the atmosphere and liked to listen to the rap sessions in the communal kitchen. Occasionally the 'vibes' were not good, but there were long periods when it was like family. It is this period I want to describe, even though, in part, it ended in tragedy.

I had rented the back room to Bill and Phyllis, a young couple who had drifted in from a small town in Texas. For a few months they had lived the life of street people, crashing at the pads of friends and acquaintances here and there; now they wanted their own pad. They soon learned how to get food stamps, where to go for free meals in Berkeley. Then they started making a few dollars selling the *Barb* and other underground papers. In the communal kitchen they listened avidly to the discussions on Vietnam, revolution, eastern philosophies, literature—whatever was going on—while they learned to smoke pot, drink wine and appreciate the virtues of wheat germ, soybeans, and other natural foods.

A tubby Japanese fellow, Sumi, occupied the front room. He had worked at many jobs, including teaching karate, and was currently part of an acting group which performed at parks and demonstrations. Sumi shared his room with a fellow who sat on the floor in the lotus position most of the day making 'god's eyes', which he sold on weekends at a flea mart in San Francisco.

The upstairs was rented to a young couple. The man, a blond guy with a warm, open countenance and a short, pointed beard, was named Christopher. About twenty-five years old, he was tall, slender and quick. His girlfriend, Helga, was slender, soft and wistful looking, with long brown hair that fell over her shoulders. She too had an appealing quality. Christopher had a B.A. in biology, but he had decided to make his living with his hands. He tinkered with cars and made furniture for the apartment. He had developed his own ideas on revolution and wrote long tracts which he tacked on walls and occasionally distributed on Telegraph Avenue.

Helga was pregnant, and Christopher soon asked if I would mind if he partitioned the upstairs landing into a small room for the baby. That was fine by me.

When I came back a couple of weeks later, I saw that the attic roof was open. He was building a sky light attic room above the space he'd partitioned. Soon after that Christopher became a problem, as he spread in all directions. He never seemed to have enough room. The small lobby downstairs became his machine shop with motors and carburetors all over the floor. He spread into the front yard where he did his carpentry. This spilled over into the driveway so that people in the rear weren't able to pull their cars in.

My mild-mannered, gentle meditator, the librarian, objected to the fact that he couldn't get into the driveway or the garage which he was renting. Christopher offered to rent the garage and make that his workshop.

The meditator said he had rented the garage because he wanted quiet and privacy, and he didn't want a noisy workshop just outside his door. Christopher found this unreasonable, and wrote me a five-page letter pointing out that the garage was not being used and he wanted to do productive work in it. It was my duty, he said, to rent it to him.

All this took place at just about the height of the activity against the war in Vietnam, and the house was fully involved in that. In fact, it was a hive of activity. The young couple who were selling the *Barb* took part in a march, and the girl got a heavy dose of tear gas. One day when I arrived and managed to penetrate the hallway to the kitchen area, I found them both on the floor of the hallway with Sumi instructing them in karate while he cooked a great pot of cabbage and meat for the household's dinner.

The 'god's eye' tenant, squatting on the floor of his room, was painting placards for the next peace march. Karl, the librarian, was kibitzing in the kitchen and drinking tea. He had a bandage on his head where a policeman had clubbed him. With him was Julian, my new tenant, pouring the tea.

Julian had arrived on a motorcycle several days before. He was short, stocky and smooth shaven, towheaded, with his hair cropped short, which was unusual in those days. His motorcycle was spotless and shining. When he asked about renting the small front room still available, his only concern was that he have a window where he could keep his eye on his bike.

Most of our people were rather untidy. When I happened to look into Julian's room a few days after he moved in, I was amazed. He had removed what little furniture there was and painted the walls bone white and the floor black. There were a few black and white prints hung, a woven mat in the center of the floor. The room had been converted into a kind of Japanese cell. Just outside the window, where he could keep his eye on it, was the shining motorcycle.

In the communal kitchen he was equally precise. He took over one shelf of the pantry. He was a lover of exotic teas, and after cleaning the pantry thoroughly, he arranged the shelf with his tea pots, cups, kettles, and exotic tea mixtures. He laid down the law: while everything else might be used in common, his tea things were not to be touched by any hands but his own.

Julian alone seemed uninterested in the political fevers of the household. He had a regular string of young girls moving through his pad. When one came, soft music, the smell of incense and the murmur of low voices drifted through the locked door.

Otherwise, Julian spent his time tinkering with his bike out front or lying almost naked on the lawn, taking in the sun. He was a sun worshipper, and very aware of his muscular chest and body. Sometimes he and Sumi wrestled in the grass. Julian also knew karate, and the practiced throws while the young couple watched them in awe.

One day I went to see Christopher about his feud with Karl. When I went upstairs to Christopher's flat I found that the extra room he had built on the landing was finished and a ladder went through the ceiling to the attic. A friend of his, Tom Campbell, a revolutionary poet with a small black beard, had moved into the new space. In the living room, Chris sat working on a piece of automobile equipment. Helga, on a mattress, sewed what looked like a large shirt.

"Chris," I said, "there's nothing I can do about the garage. Karl has rented it. He pays regularly so I can't very well ask him to give it up. You'll have to talk to him yourself."

"I *have* talked to him and he's being very stubborn. It's up to you to tell him that I need it for my work."

"You know I can't do that, Chris. He doesn't want you working in the garage because he wants peace and quiet for his meditation."

"I've offered to work in the garage only when he's not at home. He's got to give it up."

We went round and round and got nowhere.

I insisted that Chris clear his carpentry equipment out of the driveway so that it could be used for cars, and finally he agreed to do that.

About a week later, I dropped by and found a large North Vietnamese flag flying from the roof. I went to the kitchen where I found some of the clan gathered. "What," I asked, "is the idea? Who put up the flag?"

No one would say.

"We all had a part in it," Sumi finally admitted.

"But do you think this is a good idea, from a political point of view?" I asked. "Most of your neighbors are probably against the war, but they won't like to see a North Vietnamese flag flying in their neighborhood. They have sons and brothers over there."

"Well, we like the idea. We thought it would be fun."

"But it's going to bring the cops down on us, looking for dope, and the Health Department!" I said. "They'll find reasons to close the place! You'll all be in the streets and I'll go broke!"

I went to see Chris. He admitted that it was he who had put up the flag. I told him I'd have to evict him unless he took it down. He didn't promise to comply, but a couple of days later it was removed. I found it tacked to the bathroom door with a note to the landlord, saying, "We submit, but as far as we're concerned, it's still up there, flying."

The house was relatively calm for awhile. Chris had been persuaded to remove the carburetors and motors from the front entryway and was now cutting a new opening in the roof of the back bedroom, where he intended to install another skylight.

Helga's pregnancy was beginning to show. The bearded poet who was living in a newly-created room at the head of the stairs wrote revolutionary poetry which he read in the kitchen. Sumi rehearsed a play evenings. The young couple graduated from selling the *Barb* to peddling dope on Telegraph Avenue. Chris disappeared for a few days at a time, and I suspected he was their supplier.

One day Julian came to me and announced that he was moving. He said he'd sold his motorcycle, his hi-fi and some other things and was going to live at Tassajara. He wanted to become a Zen Buddhist monk.

"I've been studying Zen for some time," he said. "I've decided that's where I belong." He asked if he could store some of his things in the closet under the stairway, and I agreed.

The next day he walked off with a knapsack on his back.

A few days later, Tom, the revolutionary poet, took me aside. "I'd like to have the front room downstairs," he said. "I'm getting a little bread from my parents now, so I can pay the rent."

"Aren't you comfortable in your cubbyhole?" I asked.

"Oh, I like it a lot. It's plenty big, for me. The truth is, I've been balling Helga and Chris found out about it. He got a revolver and threatened to kill me. Imagine that! We were close friends! With all this revolutionary and communal stuff that he talks about all the time, I didn't think he'd take it that way."

"Aren't you afraid to stay around here?"

"I can't let him push me around. I'll just move downstairs and keep out of his way. Besides, Helga and I have this thing for each other. I've got to find out which way she's going to go."

Tom moved into Julian's old room. I began going over less often. The vibes weren't so good now. One day a couple of months later, I found Tom's room empty, cleared out. Sumi was in the kitchen, studying his lines for a play.

"Where's Tom?"

"He and Helga split. They're living somewhere over on Ashby."

"When?"

"About a week ago."

"How's Chris taking it?"

"Nobody ever sees him. He hardly leaves the flat."

I went upstairs and knocked. After a long time, Chris said, "Come in."

He was sitting on the mattress. No motors were being repaired. No carpentry was being done. The place was a mess.

I talked to him for awhile, tried to find the right words. I told him such things were not necessarily permanent. Helga might come back. After all, she'd be having the baby soon. It might be just a transient affair.

A few days later Sumi called me. "You'd better come over," he said. There was a pause. "Chris killed himself. Shot himself in the head."

"When?"

"A few hours ago. No one had seen him for two days. Then we heard the shot. We found him dead. Called the police. The ambulance has just taken him away."

"Has anyone let Helga know?" I managed to say through my shock.

"I know where she's living. I'll go over and tell her."

There was a puddle of blood on the floor to be cleaned up. Sumi did that. I gave him fifty dollars because I couldn't face it.

A couple of weeks later, Helga came and moved their things out. In one of Chris' drawers she found a bundle of several hundred dollars and paid the back rent.

Gradually, the shock wore off, and I rented the upstairs to two young girls. One of them was a waitress in a communal restaurant, the other drove a taxi for an alternative taxi company. I didn't realize that they were moving in with three huge sheep dogs.

One day Julian appeared. He had left the monastery.

"I got all they had to give me," he explained. "I really didn't like the life. But I still want to live a life of poverty. Besides, I have very little bread and I need to study. Would you rent me the closet where I'm storing my things?"

"You mean—to live? In that dark hole under the stairway?"

"Yes."

"How could you possibly live in there? It's got no light, no air. And you can't even stand up straight because it slopes down."

"It's enough for me."

"But it's not legal. I could get closed up for doing that."

Well, he talked and talked. Finally he persuaded me to let him try it. I charged him ten dollars a month.

He spent three days cleaning up the closet. He put several coats of whitewash on the walls, and spread his grass mat on the floor. He brought in wiring from the hall and strung up a light. At the low end of the closet he built a shelf, where he placed a few books and the hi-fi he had acquired. Then he moved in.

I could always tell when Julian was in the closet because his heavy work shoes were sitting outside.

When I asked him how it was, he said he was very comfortable.

Then one day, I came over early in the morning because the sink was stopped up. In front of the closet door I saw, neatly placed beside his boots, a pair of woman's sandals.

I fixed the sink by pouring Drano down its gullet, made up a pot of coffee, and sat down to read a book and wait for what would emerge from the closet.

The odor of the coffee must have penetrated the closet because soon Julian came, bare-chested, yawning and stretching, into the kitchen.

"Coffee?" I offered.

"Naw. I don't drink it. I'll make some tea. But it smells good."

"You move someone into the closet with you?"

"Oh, yeah. Stella. You'll meet her in a few minutes. A friend. Met her on campus. She's in the philosophy department—a graduate student."

"Isn't the place a little tight for the two of you—even if she is a graduate student?"

Later I met her—a rather plump, good-looking woman in her late twenties. At another time I learned from Julian that she was the wife of a top official for the State Department in one of the middle eastern countries—Iraq, I think. She had come back to see her parents and to complete her work at the University. Her children were with her parents.

At first the sandals appeared in front of the door just once in awhile. But soon she moved in, and they were there all the time.

Julian said she was going back to Iraq at the end of the summer, but that things were getting serious between them, and she was talking of leaving her husband to return and stay with him.

"Those kids won't fit in the closet," I warned.

After Stella left, Julian had a telephone put into the closet. It was the only telephone in the house. The telephone man must have thought it peculiar, but he installed it. Stella phoned from Iraq regularly.

Some months later, Stella reappeared. Julian left the house to be with her. I met him on Telegraph Avenue a few months later and was shocked by what I saw. He was half of what he had been. Instead of a stocky, muscular man with short, wiry hair, there was a thin, caved-in, yellow-faced ascetic with penetrating eyes and hair down to his shoulders. He was wearing sandals. We had tea, and he brought me up to date.

"Yes," he said. "Stella left her husband and came back with the children. We moved into a house and things were really groovy for awhile. But then I got restless with all those kids and left. I've gone into astrology," he continued. "Now I do horoscopes for a living. I have a little booth at the Garage on Telegraph. Come on over and see me. I'll do your horoscope, just for old times sake. Besides, I'd like to know what kind of stars watch out for landlords."

It was about then that I sold the house for twice what I'd paid for it. That's capitalism.

Seeing Julian brought back many memories of the experience with the house. One day I drove by to see what had happened to all my people.

The house looked sedate. The outside had been repainted. A new lawn was neatly trimmed, and the hedges were pruned. I knocked at the front door. A very proper middle-aged lady answered. I told her that I was the former owner and would like to see what had happened to the house.

She was the new owner. Proudly she showed me how it had been converted into a conventional duplex. It now had a real kitchen, living room and a couple of bedrooms. There were lamps, and real tables instead of boxes.

All my people were gone. I stood outside and looked at the house.

I would have welcomed a North Vietnamese flag flying from the roof.

CONTRIBUTORS

Milton Wolff has written a series of short stories collectively called *In Transit.* "The Long Ride Back" is one.

William (Boyce) Tenery, a practicing engineer licensed in Electrical, Mechanical and Control Systems, earned a degree in creative writing at the California State University at Hayward studying under Nestor Gonzalez, a well known Filipino author, and is currently working on two novels.

Elizabeth Davis has worked as a waitress, a teen educator (for Planned Parenthood) and a reporter (token white) for *Jet Magazine*. Having received her doctorate in 1980, she now teaches at the University of California, Davis. Her short stories have been published in *Mystery Magazine* and in *The San Francisco Quarterly*. She is presently writing a mystery novel.

Kathryn Winter, a Bay Area piano teacher, writes stories reminiscent of her childhood in Czechoslovakia. Her contribution to this volume is one of them. She has been published in *The Madison Review, Cricket,* and other magazines.

Robert Lee Hall is a native Californian, born in San Francisco. In the sixties he taught art and exhibited his paintings in the Bay Area. In the seventies he took up writing and published two novels, *Exit Sherlock Holmes* (Scribner's), translated into four languages, and *The King Edward Plot* (McGraw-Hill). He presently teaches advanced English classes at California High School.

Ray Faraday Nelson, and **Kirsten Nelson.** Ray, an El Cerrito fantasy novelist, won the Philip K. Dick Memorial Citation for science fiction in paperback, and the Jack London Award

for literature by a California author. He also won the Ina Cool-
brith Award for serious poetry. His science-fiction novel
Dimension of Horror will soon appear in a French translation
from Librairie Plon of Paris. **Kirsten,** beloved wife of Ray,
made her national writing debut in the first issue of the
science fiction magazine *The Last Wave* with a memoir of
Philip K. Dick.

Marko Fong is 28 and has managed thus far to escape the
practice of law by devoting himself to his first novel, *The Story
of a California Chinese Family*. He is a graduate of Stanford
and Boalt Hall, lives in Oakland with his stockbroker and dog,
has too much stereo equipment and visits his mother "not
often enough."

Lili Artel was born on a Thursday so she knew she had far to
go. She got from New York City to the California Bay Area
where her stories have appeared in all three *Thursday's Child*
collections. She has also published a book of poems *I Come
From A Long Line of Tenants,* and creates fiber sculptures.

Jean MacKellar lived in Paris for many years, observing
French ways. She has sometimes used French aphorisms as
the basis for her short stories. At present she lives in an old
brown shingle house near the University of California campus,
studying the inhabitants of Berkeley.

Clay Fulghum was strongly influenced by the writers who met
at Ray Nelson's house in the early days of the group. The
stubbornness, scrappiness and strength of the women in her
native South inspired the piece included here. Clay presently
lives in Atlanta.

Roselore Fox left her native Germany at age fifteen to roam
Europe for ten years. She supported herself as a gourmet cook
through skills acquired in Switzerland, Austria and Italy. In
1959 she came to the United States. Haunted by memories of
her childhood, she began writing. Her first novel *The Civilian*
is now being evaluated by New York publishing houses.

Bruce Kaiper is co-curator of an international exhibit entitled "The Other America: History, Art and Culture of the American Labor Movement" that is travelling in Europe and will come to the United States in 1985. He also served as historical advisor for the new documentary film "Seeing Red."

Conrad Montell began reveries as Don Quixote of East Harlem. After careers as engineer, computer analyst and Gepetto the wood craftsman, he returns to writing with a dream of translating his radical/humanist/romantic vision into at least one statement which is artistic and not a cliché.

Ruth Heineck Broek helped her parents pioneer a homestead in the Okanogan highlands of the Colville Indian Reservation where her father built schools and churches and established communities. Later she married a geographer from Holland. With him she lived abroad for many years and travelled to distant and exotic lands.

Lee Ann Johnson lives with her husband, Don, in Pleasanton, California and writes full time. Her first book, a biography, was published in 1980. She is currently at work on a novel.

Dexter Mast weighed twice as much as most babies at birth and was exhibited at the county fair. Today he is a retired sergeant of the Oakland police with thirty-two years of experience behind the police stories which he writes. The spelling in his stories improved, he says, when he acquired a sleep-in dictionary: he married another member of the Thursday's Child group.

Richard Gold teaches composition at community colleges in Washington and works for a publisher which produces books on the psychology and education of the special child. Since he left the Bay Area, he also been writing kids' mystery stories.

Gwen Jordan, a pleasure seeker of sorts, spends much of her free time pursuing her special interests which include: handcrafts with a preference for knitting, playing with her dogs, model railroads and committing fantasies to paper. Pragmatically, she is a Probation Officer working in a felony investigation unit.

Virginia Ruiz Seiden, formerly an actress and singer, was born in Mexico. She wrote radio scripts and a newspaper column in Mexico City before being hired as a Spanish writer-publicist by Twentieth Century Fox Studios in New York. She has written a historical novel in English, and several short stories, which she is revising with the help and inspiration of the Thursday's Child group.

Marlin Spike Werner is a specialist in treating disorders of hearing and speech and is half owner of the Lafayette Hearing Aid Center in Lafayette, naturally.

Nina Zeitler Clark, born in South Dakota, has been a Californian since 1959. A feature journalist professionally, she began to write short stories and poetry in addition to her newspaper work, after wandering into a fiction class by mistake. This is her second fiction piece.

Clara Robbin, a teacher for many years, still substitutes in the Berkeley schools. She has published both fiction and non-fiction in the national magazines, *The Instructor* and *The Pointer*. Her stories also appeared in Thursday's Child volumes II and III. With her husband, Ed Robbin, she has hosted the weekly meetings of the Thursday night workshop for many years.

Edward Robbin, founder and editor of the first three collections of Thursday's Child stories, was leader of the Thursday night gatherings until his death in April, 1983. The author of *Woody Guthrie and Me, Birth,* and many short stories, he had a varied career as a journalist, actor, general contractor, and *chalutz* in pre-Israel Palestine. He became well known as a local radio personality for his interviews and readings of stories on KPFA.